I0708555

Scarecrows

and

Corpses

A Meadowood Mystery

Book 1

Nancy M. Wade

Scarecrows and Corpses is a work of fiction. Names, characters, places, and incidents either are the product of the author's imagination based on some historical real events or are used fictitiously. Any resemblance to actual persons, living or dead, events or locales is entirely coincidental.

This book is protected under the copyright laws of the United States of America. Any reproduction or unauthorized use of the material or artwork contained herein is prohibited without the express written permission of Nancy M. Wade.

Published in the United States by
GARNAN Enterprises, LLC of Ohio.

Copyright 2020 by Nancy M. Wade
2nd Edition 2022
3rd Edition May 2023
All Rights Reserved.

ISBN - 978-1737699897

Works of Nancy M. Wade

Meadowood Mysteries Series:
Scarecrows and Corpses – book 1
Reunion With Death – book 2
Deadly Bones – book 3
Berry Little Murder – book 4

Circle-D Saga Trilogy:
Endless Circle – book 1
Moment in Time – book 2
Gun for Hire – book 3 *coming in 2023

Reflections: A Sentimental Journey

Frontier Heart

Courtship of Laura

REVIEWS

Scarecrows and Corpses:

Scarecrows and Corpses is an intriguing and fun read for all the cozy mystery fans out there! I wanted to read it in one sitting, but alas, bedtime called, and I had to wait until the next evening to finish. The story was just that good. Meredith is a very relatable main character with a cast of solid supporting characters readers will enjoy. The well-written description of Meadowood and its citizens made me feel like I lived there. Plus, the tension leading up to the discovery of the "one who did the dastardly deed" was truly entrancing. I want more! I cannot wait for the next Meadowood Mystery.
 Author: T. Robinson-Smith, *Ivy Creek Sewing Circle*

Loved this mystery! I made the mistake of reading late at night and was up most of the night finishing it. I can usually figure out "whodunit" but not this time!
 Alsbarb – Amazon 9/30/2020

Great mystery story. Loved all the characters and a small town community. Good read!
 H. Amme on Goodreads

Scarecrows and Corpses

A Meadowood Mystery

Book 1

Table of Contents

Chapter 1

Wisps of fog shrouded low-lying areas of ground as I drove toward the park and the scout jamboree being held there. The brisk October morning still held the chill from the night before, but rays of bright sunlight pierced the scattered clouds and promised to warm the land and burn away the fog remnants.

I parked in the gravel lot and hurried to my den's campsite; the bright blue pennant that we erected yesterday waved proudly as it marked our den. The boys sat around the campfire circle, finishing their breakfasts or rubbing frigid hands near the warm flames.

Ted Williams, the assistant den leader, greeted me as I approached. "Hey there, Merry. The boys are chomping at the bit to get to the corn maze before the other scouts."

I smiled and nodded in agreement. Ted was a nice guy, friendly and helpful. He was well liked around town; running his own real estate office as both an agent and developer. He had sold me my house ten years ago and since then we've been close friends, he and his wife Barbara and their son Joey. I watched as he gathered up cooking utensils, then doused the fire with water. Embers hissed as smoke rose into the still damp air.

"How'd it go last night?" I asked Ted.

"Great, no problems."

I turned to the boys in various stages of breakfast, "Pack up all of your belongings and place your backpacks inside your tents. When we get back from the corn maze, we'll take down the tents and prepare to leave. Your parents should be here by then," I instructed my cub scouts.

Ted and I gave the boys a few more minutes to finish their chores, checked to make sure the fire was completely extinguished, then told everyone to line up by two's.

Seven and nine-year-old boys' excited and giggling voices filled the morning air. Everyone talked at once as my cub scouts marched the mile and a half from Fox Run Park to the Granger corn maze. I saw three other dens walking the trail behind us as we all headed to the fun Halloween activity.

I loved this time of year. The fall colors were breathtaking, and the air had just enough of a nip to it to make a person step lively. I think I was as excited as the boys; I always looked forward to this annual event of exploring the Granger Farm corn maze.

Acres of tall corn grew in the fields to our left; the stalks now dry and brown, ready for harvest. Ears of corn already filled three towering stainless-steel silos for winter feed and now the remaining stalks and leaves were ready to cut for cattle forage and to prepare the soil for next year's planting. Adjacent acres glistened with morning dew, glowed golden in the morning sunshine with rows of dried soybean plants that undulated in the brisk air. A brick red barn with a gambrel roof occupied the land west of the house; its wide doors were propped open with bales of hay. The weathered barn sported a faded *Mail Pouch Tobacco* sign; painted on so many rural structures. Tethered horses snickered in their stalls, hoping for apple treats from the groups of children that raced into the barn. The long pig building sat downwind, east of the main farmhouse, barn and chicken coop, its sturdy metal roofing and walls allowed a mixture of sun and shade with ample ventilation in the divided pens. I could hear the hogs snorting and grunting in their pens as I hiked toward the corn maze.

A pair of colorful scarecrows dressed in ragged clothing guarded the entrance to the maze. One had a pumpkin head with a wide, gay smile; the other scarecrow's pumpkin head leered with carved, sinister jagged teeth. A shudder went through me as I viewed the head worthy of a Stephen King horror story.

I walked directly to the small admission booth manned by one of the farm employees and paid the fee for our cub scout den to enter the maze. Ted would wait near the exit of the maze to corral our boys as each finished. I planned to stay by the entrance, keeping a head count and in case any of the boys got turned around or came back out. The scarecrows would keep me company.

"Have fun, take your time. Call out if you get lost or can't find your way out. Mr. Williams and I are right here to help you. Okay?" I asked as I scanned the expectant faces.

Several heads nodded and others mumbled yes as they jostled each other, eager to begin. I laughed, then checked my wristwatch for the time.

3

With a clap of my hands, I shouted, "Okay; one, two, three, go!"

The boys scrambled and ran into the intricate labyrinth. I listened to the rustle of brittle corn stalks as they moved along the paths, twisting and turning back and forth. I recognized the distinct voices laughing and calling out; boys I had guided as den mother for over two years. They were as familiar to me as my own sons.

All of a sudden, a scream rang out. I knew that voice only too well - my son, Billy. It was not a scream of delight, but one filled with terror. I dropped my backpack and dashed into the leafy maze. My mother's antennae ramped up as I followed the sound. My child needed help; I didn't think of any danger to myself as I sprinted into the unknown.

The maze turned left and right; twice I ran into a solid wall and had to turn around, seeking my way.

"Billy! Where are you? I'm coming," I yelled.

"Here I am," he cried.

The corn stalks muffled his voice. I stopped and tried again to get my bearings before plowing ahead. Where were the others? Was Billy hurt? I tried not to panic as I sought his location.

"Don't move. I'm almost there," I called.

I turned a corner in the maze and suddenly saw him crouched on the ground with his hands covering his face. My older son Johnny crashed through a wall of corn and reached his brother just as I did. He saw me at the same time.

"I'm sorry, Mom. I tried to find him, but he got behind," Johnny said as he wiped at threatening tears.

"It's all right. I'm here now." I gathered both of my boys in a fierce hug then ran my hands over arms and legs, searching for signs of injury on Billy. My attention was solely on him.

"Billy, look at me," I said, as I gently pulled his hands down from his face. "What happened?"

He sobbed and hugged me tighter, then raised his hand to point at the trail ahead. I stared intently where he directed and gasped aloud.

"Oh my God. Both of you stay right here."

A man's body lay crumpled face down between the rows of corn. I slowly edged closer. A metallic smell stung my nostrils. Blood flooded the ground beneath the man's head, his face was turned and pressed into the loose dirt. I stooped to study the body. I gently reached inside the collar of a bloody flannel shirt and pressed two fingertips against his neck, seeking a pulse. I found none but tried again. The pale skin contained bluish discolorations on the neck, almost the same shade of blue as his denim overalls. I stood, shaking badly, then turned away from the ghastly sight.

My hand on my heart, I stifled a scream as Ted Williams suddenly exploded between the close corn stalks, his shirt splattered red. I stepped back in a panic and nearly tripped on a large shovel that lay nearby; it was covered in blood and dirt. What had happened here?

The noise of the other boys nearing our spot in the maze brought my focus back to the matter at hand. I hurried back to where I had left Billy and Johnny and moved them before the other boys joined us. No one else should see this gruesome sight.

"Johnny, do you think you can find your way back out to the entrance? Can you do that? Take the boys and wait for me."

"What are you going to do?" Johnny stammered, trembling.

"I'm going to call your father. I'll be all right. All of you scouts need to turn around," I directed in a loud voice to the group of boys still making their way through the maze.

I heard confused mumbling and questions as to what was going on from the scouts, but they obeyed my command. Johnny clutched Billy's hand in a steel grip that I knew would not be broken as he held his younger brother and led the group. I was never more proud of him.

My hands shook as I fumbled for my cell phone in my jacket pocket and quickly punched in my husband's number.

"Hello." I heard the warm, confidant voice on the other end of the line.

"Douglas, come quick. We found a body," I cried into the phone.

"What? Where?" he questioned, his tone of voice instantly professional and in command.

"In the corn maze; it's horrible. Hurry."

"Are you and the boys all right?"

"We're okay, just shaken. I don't know what to do," I said.

"Don't touch anything. I'll be right there. Deputies are on the way."

I hung up and wrapped my arms around my middle to still my own quaking. I slowly made my way back toward the front of the maze to huddle with my sons and the other boys in my den. I didn't search to see what had happened to Ted. Within minutes, sirens blared and strobes of red and blue flashing lights atop police cruisers filled the farmyard as the sheriff and his deputies arrived, my husband among them.

His long strides brought him to our side in seconds, and he engulfed the boys and me in one large group hug. He held my face between his hands and gazed into my eyes.

"Are you sure you're okay?" Doug asked as he pressed a kiss on the forehead of each son and hugged them again.

"Yes. Go do what you need to do. I've got to take these boys back to our campsite and see that they get home safely."

"The office will need to take an official statement from you about what you saw and did. Can you tell me anything else?"

I started to shake my head no, then paused and thought of Ted.

"Um, Ted Williams was there too. He had blood on his shirt," I remembered, as the sight of him filled my mind.

"We'll take it from here," Doug said.

"How could something like this happen here?" I thought as I watched my husband join the sheriff and the other deputies to begin their investigation.

"Who was it?" I whispered to myself.

My mind replayed all the events of the past week as I agonized for an answer. Nothing like this ever happened in our tiny town.

Chapter 2

Meadowood is a typical, small Midwestern town. We are within driving distance to several big cities within the state and an hour away from the state capital, but still a rural community. Central Ohio is a mixture of rolling hills dotted with century old towns and surrounded by rich farmlands that make you feel like you've stepped back in time.

My name is Meredith Gardner and I don't think I'd rather live anywhere else. It's a town filled with caring people who look after each other and take pride in knowing everyone's business - maybe too much at times. Still, you have to admire the quaint buildings and store fronts that line the main street through town. We have our florist and butcher shops, one Knox Savings and Loan office and a branch of Wells Fargo Bank, the usual insurance and real estate offices mixed in with various commercial businesses; all situated in brick and clapboard structures donning gables or dormers that date back at least a hundred years. A few buildings were marked with the status of historic landmarks by the state of Ohio.

I was on my way home from a morning of shopping; bags of groceries and Halloween treats filled the back of my older, apple red Dodge minivan with its rusty bumper and quarter panels, compliments of too many icy winters and salty roads. It wasn't the best-looking vehicle on the road, but the engine hummed like a sewing machine and the van seated plenty of kids, including the occasional scout troop.

As I waited for the traffic light to turn green, I admired the array of colors decorating the oak and maple trees lining Park Avenue. The fall colors this year were so vibrant – crimson, gold, and burnt orange leaves fluttered in the crisp autumn breeze. Who needs to travel to Vermont, or even the Appalachian Mountains, when the Ohio countryside provided such breathtaking scenery? I cracked my car window and breathed in the cool fall air. I smelled a whiff of burning wood from someone's fireplace. In the next block, I smiled to myself as I spied slim spirals of smoke rising above the chimney of Joseph Cooper's home.

I drove slowly as I neared Frannie's Frocks and waved to the owner standing out front - my aunt, Frances Andrews. Aunt Fran has the best dress shop in town stocked with the latest fashion trends. She smiled at me and waved back, then pointed to her wristwatch as a reminder to me; we had a meeting to attend later. I waved again to indicate that I got the message.

A few minutes later, I turned down our road located toward the edge of town. Maple Drive dead-ended into our driveway with nothing but a cornfield and woods beyond it. Normally a quiet, low traffic street, it was a blessing to have some place where my boys were safe riding their bikes or simply playing ball outside. I remember thinking what a perfect location it was when we first bought the cozy, older, two-story colonial ten years ago. The white siding needed a good power-washing and my eyes focused on the chipped window trim that could stand a coat of paint, but it was home. I parked the car and opened the side door into the mudroom before returning to unload the trunk and lug it all into the house. Sunlight streamed onto the newly renovated kitchen's speckled granite counters above driftwood gray cabinets. The pale slate and taupe colors of the tile backsplash sparkled as light poured through the glass French doors of the adjoining dining room. The kitchen felt warm and homey; I could still smell the oatmeal and cinnamon that lingered from our morning breakfast.

I was greeted warmly by a meow and furry presence winding his way through my legs as I tried to stack groceries on the counter.

"Thank you, I missed you too. I hope you've been a good boy and left those birds alone. I better not find any feathers on the back porch if you want your treats," I told our orange and white tabby cat, Mittens, as I bent to stroke his back and give his head a knuckle rub.

Mittens arched his back and flicked his tail as if in answer to my admonitions, then meowed again as he stood by his empty food bowl. He waited patiently on me as he groomed his long hair with a wet paw, dragging it across his nose and eyes like a washcloth. I always found a cat's behavior so interesting; what gave them that instinct and mannerism?

I gave him another affectionate pet as I filled his bowl and freshened his water and was rewarded with a loud purr. I could always count on Mittens to greet me during the day when the house was empty and seemed so lonely with the boys in school and my husband Doug at work. He ruled the roost at times; an integral part of our family since he had first been weaned at six weeks old. Mittens would sit and listen to me when others never had the time, and I found myself talking to the cat and using him for a sounding board more and more. Was that strange? I didn't think so. I'm sure he understood exactly what I said.

Groceries all put up, I checked the clock and saw I had two hours before my sons would be home from school. Good. Plenty of time to write up my current Avon business orders and review the latest campaign products to sell to my customers. I enjoyed visiting with neighbors and friends as I walked the route my Avon sales' district had assigned to me for Meadowood. I normally planned one full day to walk about, deliver new campaign books, take orders from customers and listen to the latest gossip in town. Cosmetic sales gave me my own personal income and a sense of independence; I didn't have to feel guilty about splurging on a new pair of shoes or treating myself to a salon visit if I used money that I had earned and not the household budget. Flipping through the booklet's pages, I made a few notes about some new fragrances and a nail polish color that I was certain some of my ladies would like. Maybe tomorrow would be a good day to visit my Avon customers; I'll add it to the calendar and my to-do list.

"Looks like my weekly calendar is getting pretty full", I noted as I penciled in Wednesday as an Avon day. "How do I get wrapped up in so many committees?” I asked Mittens. “Oh well, I’ll manage somehow.”

Mittens meowed and jumped up onto the stool next to me. He butted his head against my arm as if to show he had complete confidence in me to juggle my busy life. He stretched and settled himself as his tail swished back and forth between the chair legs.

I patted him absent-mindedly as I turned my thoughts to dinner plans and mentally inventoried what was in the freezer that I could add to today’s fresh vegetable purchases. A menu in mind, I scooped up my Avon folder and stashed it in the kitchen desk drawer that I had allocated for my business.

I had just finished seasoning a small chicken and shoved it into the oven to roast, when I heard the kitchen door open.

“Mom! I’m home,” announced my seven-year-old son, Billy. He dumped his school bag onto the bench next to the side door and kicked off his sneakers, laces still tied, and immediately headed to the cookie jar.

“Just one,” I said automatically and wondered how many times I had repeated that mantra. “Where’s your brother?”

“Johnny stopped at Joey William’s house. He said he wouldn’t stay long.”

“All right. Do you have any homework?”

“Nope. Mister Housewright told us we got all our work done in class today,” Billy said proudly.

13

"Well, that's good. Why don't you take some time to work on your Cub Scout project before our meeting this week? You'll be ahead of everyone," I suggested.

"Can't I wait until Johnny is home to help me?" whined Billy.

"No, it's your project, not your brother's. You can at least get it started before you ask for his help."

"Aww Mom, sometimes it's not fair having your mother as your den leader. I bet the other boys don't have to do their work alone."

"Sorry, buddy, but that's life. Now take that poster board and some magic markers and think of how you want to arrange your variety of leaves and tree names." I handed him another cookie to sweeten my words and pushed him in the right direction. I had to shake my head as I watched him trudge up the stairs, dragging the poster board behind him, banging it on the top of each step. The edges of the board will be crimped by the time he gained his room.

I sighed, "Oh well. Someday he'll appreciate all the things I do."

"Hi Mom," called Johnny an hour later as he quietly entered the kitchen, placed his backpack on the bench and reached for an apple from the bowl on the table. "Did Billy tell you I stopped by Joey's house? He got a new bike; it's really cool."

"Yes, he did. How was school?"

Johnny was my studious and reserved son; he often preferred to sit and listen, to observe people and actions going on around him. He was nine years old going on thirty; overly mature for his age. I could always depend on him to lend a hand with chores or look after his younger brother. Between the two boys, I think my Johnny favored his father more than me; not just his dark brown hair and hazel colored eyes, but his sense of responsibility too – so like Doug.

"School's okay. The guys are all talking about the big scout jamboree this weekend. Is Mister Williams still camping out with us?"

"As far as I know. I'm counting on him to sleep over with you boys. I'll be at the jamboree in the daytime as den mother, but Ted will sleep overnight. He volunteered even though his business keeps him very busy, so I hope you guys won't give him any trouble."

"Mother, of course we'll be on our best behavior; scout's honor," joked Johnny as he tossed his apple core into the trash can and helped himself to a glass of milk and a cookie before heading upstairs.

"I hope Ted Williams knows what he's getting into," I told Mittens as I simmered a pan of green beans on the stove and started peeling potatoes. "I'm afraid our scouts might have some antics planned."

"Rowww," Mittens agreed, as he flicked his tail then padded over to the back door and squeezed through the pet flap to go outdoors onto the rear deck.

I watched a pair of startled robins take flight; the bird feeder swinging on its shepherd hook. I had a feeling that Mittens was responsible for that. I told Doug to hang that thing higher where the cat couldn't swat at it. *"Oh well,"* I sighed again.

Dinner was almost ready as I set the table and called to the boys to wash up when I heard my husband's car pull into the driveway. I

15

smiled at him as he strode into our cozy kitchen and gave me a quick kiss on the cheek.

"Mmm, something smells good. What's for supper?" Douglas Gardner asked as he placed his cap on a coat hook, unbuckled his deputy's Sam Brown belt and removed his service revolver.

He unlocked the gun cabinet that stood in the corner of my laundry room and placed his gun in the cabinet, out of harm's way and little hands. He never failed to complete this routine safety procedure before joining the family. I nodded in approval and watched him as he walked to the kitchen sink to wash his own hands. He looked so handsome in his sheriff deputy's uniform; my eyes couldn't get enough of him.

"Have a good day?" I asked. "Catch all the bad guys and keep our city safe?"

"Yeah sure, as if this town ever had any excitement. Gave out two speeding tickets and one warning for littering; does that count?" Doug asked.

I laughed at his cynical expression. "Someday you'll regret those words. Thought you liked our town?"

"I do. Don't get me wrong. It's just that most days are so boring; how am I ever going to impress the boss with my investigative skills if nothing ever happens here?" Doug complained.

"Well, I like our quiet life and community. I wouldn't want to live in a place where I didn't feel safe walking about," I stated.

"No, you're right, of course. I'm just letting off steam. Where are the boys?"

"Upstairs. You better go check on them; they're awfully quiet up there. And make sure they washed up for dinner so we can eat."

"Yes ma'am," Doug said as he gave me a mock salute.

Our schedules were all so erratic, but I insisted that dinner was family time and we all share the meal together regardless of meetings or sporting events pulling us elsewhere.

Doug carved the chicken while I served portions of vegetables on each plate and poured the boys each a fresh glass of cold milk. We held hands and bowed our heads to say grace before everyone dug in and began talking at once between mouthfuls of food.

"Johnny, don't talk with your mouth full. Billy, please chew with your mouth closed. Thank you," I admonished as I passed the biscuits.

Doug raised an eyebrow but said nothing as I watched him try to swallow before he joined the conversation.

"Aren't we eating earlier than usual?" he asked.

"A bit, but I've got a committee meeting tonight with Aunt Fran."

"What is it this time?" Doug inquired.

"I promised her I'd help organize the charity food drive for Thanksgiving to benefit the homeless in the county. We only have thirty days, you know. Thanksgiving will be here before you know it," I explained, trying not to show my annoyance with him.

I'm certain I mentioned the food drive to him last week when we were discussing the holidays and if his parents or mine would be here for dinner. My mom and dad, Bill and Margaret Johnson, lived in Meadowood but they were snowbirds who took off for winter months spent in the warm Florida sunshine. Doug's parents lived up in Shaker Heights, a two-hour drive away, near Lake Erie in one of the upscale neighborhoods. I know Harold and Maude Gardner loved me and the kids, but they seemed to take a particular delight in reminding Doug that he married beneath himself because I didn't finish college. Inviting either set of parents for a special holiday occasion or visit required advance coordination. We did discuss the subject. Men... in one ear and out the other!

"Yeah, okay. The boys and me can shoot some baskets before bedtime. You won't be too long, will you?" asked Doug.

"I don't think so, but you never know. I'll try to be back before eight," I said.

I hurried to clear the table, put away leftovers and packed the dishwasher. I ran my fingers through my hair to fluff up the short curls before scooping up my notebook and purse, then headed for the door.

"Don't I get a kiss good-bye?" asked Doug as I turned to leave.

"Of course," I said as I hurried to plant a quick kiss on his cheek and one on each of the boy's foreheads. "You guys have fun. I'll tuck you into bed as soon as I get back."

"Bye Mom," a chorus of voices sang as I headed down the drive on my way to Aunt Fran's house.

Chapter 3

I recognized several familiar faces in Aunt Fran's living room as I entered her cottage home. I smiled and nodded; greeted different women as I made my way back to the kitchen to see if my aunt needed help to serve the coffee and tea.

"Hey there. How many people are you expecting tonight?" I asked my aunt as I arranged cups and saucers on a tray.

"Hmm, maybe fifteen, not everyone's here yet. Take that tray in, won't you? I'll bring in this one," Aunt Fran said, lifting a tray arranged with plates of oatmeal cookies and golden biscotti.

"Those look good," I commented as I carried the cups of hot coffee and tea.

"Picked them up at Martha's bakery this afternoon. I probably gained five pounds just drooling over them," Aunt Fran said as she tucked a strand of shoulder-length hair behind an ear.

"Oh, I doubt it."

A widow, Aunt Fran was still an attractive woman; her dark blond hair streaked with a few gray strands, the only sign of her advancing years. She worked out at the YWCA once a week, and with her busy schedule running the dress shop; I was certain she burned more than enough calories to keep her girlish figure. I always thought I favored my aunt more than my mother since we had the same coloring–both dark blonds with a blue-gray eye color. Unfortunately, I think I inherited more of my mother's body shape than my aunt's. I have to be constantly on my guard and count calories that seem to paste themselves directly on my hips and thighs. My dear husband, Doug, always reassures me he likes my figure and womanly curves, but I have eyes and a mirror. My weight is a never-ending battle that I feared I was losing.

Three more women arrived and greeted everyone warmly as they found seats grouped about the comfortable room, decorated in shades of soft turquoise and chocolate brown. Some of these gals were Avon customers of mine, two others were mothers of cub scouts in my den. I served the beverages and went back into the kitchen for a second tray of drinks, then placed them on the square coffee table.

"Thanks for helping out, Merry. Okay, ladies, shall we get started?" Aunt Fran said as she called the meeting to order.

"Martha, are these cookies from your bakery?" asked Donna Simon as she reached for a napkin and biscotti.

"Yes, we just baked this batch a few hours ago," whispered Martha.

"Ladies, may I have your attention, please? We need to discuss how and where we can hold our annual charity food drive. I'm looking for some ideas. We really need to get this thing off the ground by next week if we expect to have a decent turnout. Thanksgiving is only four weeks away," stated Aunt Fran.

"Can we hold it in the school again?" asked Donna.

20

"What about enlisting the fire station in the food drive? They've got lots of storage space and could be a good collection point," suggested Anna Thompson, one of my Avon customers and a close friend of my aunt.

"Carol, can you speak with your husband Pete about the drive? He's a fireman; maybe he can get permission from the chief for a collection box," I said.

Carol Goodwin is a petite gal with a ready smile, sparkling blue eyes and dark brunette hair; she's usually willing to pitch in with cub scout projects involving her son Bryan. She nodded to me as she glanced about the room.

"Well, I can mention it to him and see what he says," Carol said.

"Great. I think the fire station would work better than the school for this. It's in the center of town and easily accessible and we won't have to worry about students helping themselves to snacks like they did last year," stated Aunt Fran.

"Are we planning on making up meals and serving them in the church or just donating to the food bank?" inquired Georgia Simmons. Georgia is a robust woman, slightly rotund, and it always surprises me when I hear her speak in such a squeaky, high pitched voice that sounds like Minnie Mouse. That tiny voice contrasted with her large body. Georgia is also the wife of our local sheriff and has served as president of the Meadowood School PTA for five years. I've worked with her on the PTA and other projects. I do always try to stay on the good side of Georgia since her husband is my husband's boss. Even small towns have politics.

"I think we will probably need to donate to the food bank and shelter. They can add the canned goods or packaged items we collect to their inventory. It might be too difficult to assemble meals based upon what we receive," said Aunt Fran.

"Let's start by making some posters and place them around town to announce the food drive. I'll be glad to distribute them if I can get help with the design and printing," I offered.

Barbara Williams raised her hand to gain our attention. "My office can run off some flyers on our color printer. Just give me the basic facts and I'll put something together on a PowerPoint slide."

"That would be great. Thanks, Barb. As soon as we know if we can use the fire station, I'll call you. I guess we just need to list the dates, maybe November first through the twenty-third, and a brief description of the purpose," Aunt Fran explained.

Barbara smiled and nodded in agreement.

I liked Barbara Williams; she was really a sweet person and so attractive with her short ginger hair and fair complexion. For the life of me, I don't know why she and her husband Ted got divorced. Sometimes it was a bit awkward for me dealing with Ted as my assistant scout leader and then dealing with Barb as one of my customers. Sort of put me in the middle more than once when an issue came up with their son Joey, especially since he is the best friend of my Johnny.

Now that we had sketched our plans, most of the women broke into smaller groups. The room buzzed like bees in a beehive as the ladies chattered and enjoyed their coffee and treats. I tried to mingle and moved about the room, refilled cups and collected empty paper plates.

"I'll be stopping by tomorrow, Anna. I've got a new Avon book for you and that bottle of *Topaz* cologne. Oh, Carol, wait until you see the hot pink nail polish being offered in this campaign. You're going to love it," I announced in my best cosmetic sales pitch.

I half listened to snatches of conversation as I walked back and forth between the kitchen and parlor.

"I hear developers want the Granger farm..."

"No! I didn't know it was up for sale."

"...hmm, sheriff sale... I'm not sure I like a giant mall being built on the edge of town."

"Wonder what Fred will do now."

"Guess who I saw coming out of Betty's diner over in Pottstown, Friday night? It was close to midnight, and he wasn't alone either," whispered one of Aunt Fran's neighbors.

"There'll be hell to pay if they get caught. She's got an awfully jealous husband," her friend mumbled.

I paused as I loaded my tray, hoping to hear more of this interesting tidbit, but the two women abruptly stopped speaking when they noticed me lingering, then glared at me. I pasted a half smile on my face and moved on. Their comments piqued my curiosity. I needed

23

to corner my aunt later and see if she knows whom they were talking about.

I gave myself a mental shake as I set the tray down on the kitchen counter and started loading the dishwasher for my aunt. I'm becoming as bad a gossip as those old biddies in there. Shame on me! Still, it was awfully interesting, and heaven knows, nothing interesting ever happens in Meadowood. A person could die of boredom.

A half hour later, I entered the house to the sound of my phone ringing on the kitchen counter. I snatched it up and said hello before the caller could hang up.

"Merry, I need you to do me a favor," Colleen Callahan said breathlessly on the other end of the line. Colleen is the principal of the Meadowood Elementary School where my boys go and has been my absolute best friend since second grade when her folks moved into town down the street from mine. We grew up together, had braces on our teeth together, went to Knox Community College together, and double dated together. Even though Colleen went on to further her education at the University of Michigan and I got married, we are still closer than sisters. I'd do anything for her, and she'd do the same.

"What is it?" I asked.

24

"Sally Granville is sick; I need a teacher's assistant on Thursday morning to help in Mrs. Klausson's kindergarten class. Can you do it?" Colleen begged.

"Of course, I can. I have some stuff I have to do to get ready for our scout jamboree this weekend, but I'll juggle some things around. You can count on me to be there Thursday. Is the class doing anything special that day? Do I need to bring anything?"

"I believe Mrs. Klausson is decorating pumpkins for Halloween with finger paint. You might want to wear old clothes or at least an apron," laughed Colleen.

"Sounds like fun. Oh hey, while I have you on the line, how about coming to dinner Friday night with Doug and I?"

"This Friday? Just the three of us or are you trying to fix me up with someone again? I know how that devious mind of yours works, Merry Gardner," Colleen joked.

"Okay, I confess, Doug did ask me if he could have his friend Ron Wythe come over. You know Ron; he's a good guy. I think he likes you too," I admitted.

"Yeah, sure he's a good guy if you like the big muscular jock type. All he ever talks about is football," exclaimed Colleen, exasperated.

"So, you'll come?" I asked, not wanting to take no for an answer.

"I guess I have to since you're doing me a favor on Thursday, but he better not brag about his Buckeyes and how they will beat my Wolverines next month. You know how devoted I am to my alma mater."

25

"What can I say? The guys are gung-ho when it comes to OSU football. Ron and Doug can't help being die hard Buckeye supporters, especially since they both graduated from OSU and Ron was on the football team.   You know how it is; everyone in this state looks forward to the big game between the Buckeyes and Michigan in November. It's a tradition. If the guys begin talking football, I promise I'll take your side if that will make you feel better," I cajoled.

"All right. What time on Friday?" asked Colleen.

"How about six-thirty? My boys are going to their grandparent's house for a sleep-over, so we'll get to have a nice, quiet, adult dinner party."

"Fine. Thanks for filling in on Thursday."

"No problem. See you at school," I said as I hung up. I grabbed a pencil and updated my wall calendar to show Thursday volunteer time and Friday's dinner party time. I couldn't cope without my calendar or notebook keeping my life straight.

Chapter 4

The sun shone brightly on one of those rare, warm autumn days. Ohio's seasonal weather has been accused of changing from hour to hour to the frustration of both visitors and residents, but if you live here long enough, you learn to appreciate the sunny days and bundle up for the cold ones. I strolled through my neighborhood, dropping off Avon campaign books and knocking on doors. I carried a tote bag stuffed with new campaign books, my order pad and pen, plus several bags of customer orders that required delivery.

Carol Goodwin greeted me warmly as I delivered the order to her eager, outstretched hand. She smiled and welcomed me into her sunny yellow kitchen. I inhaled the smell of freshly brewed coffee and sniffed appreciatively at the beef pot roast simmering in the crock pot.

"Mmm, smells good in here," I said.

"How about a cup of coffee?" asked Carol as she searched through the Avon package. "Oh good, glad you found that lipstick I wanted."

"No problem," I said as I poured a mug of the steaming coffee. "That pink shade is out of stock now, but I called around and one of the other gals in my sales' district had it on hand. I traded her for it. We do it all the time."

"Thanks. I can always count on you, Merry."

"Wait until you see the new nail polish that would match that lipstick; it'll be perfect with your coloring."

"Go ahead and order one for me. I'll look through the book later to see if I need anything else. I just love that ruby red glassware; maybe I can find a piece on sale to add to my collection. Oh hey, Pete told me that the chief said it would be okay for us to use the station for our food drive."

"Great. I'll let Aunt Fran know, then Barb and I can write up the flyers with the location," I said.

"Pete told me that someone from the committee has to stop by and make the final arrangements with the chief, but otherwise, it's all set," Carol explained.

"Okay. I can do that or Aunt Fran. Tell Pete thanks for me, will you? I've gotta run. Thanks for the coffee too."

"See you this weekend," called Carol as I started down the steps. I waved to her and continued to my next stop.

The afternoon hours went quickly as I dropped off some books in mailboxes for customers that worked during the day or enjoyed brief visits with several of my other ladies. I strolled down Park Avenue and stopped in a few of the small gift shops, reminding the owners of the upcoming food drive plus handed out my Avon campaign book for some of the salesgirls.

I saved my last delivery for Anna Thompson since her house was located closest to mine. I knocked twice and waited before I heard her slow footsteps crossing hardwood floors as she approached the front door.

"Howdy Merry," she drawled in that Texan accent of hers that ranged from slightly southern to downright Texan cowhand. Anna grew up on a panhandle cattle ranch outside Abilene and lived most of her life there until her husband Chuck had to transfer with his job to Columbus or be forced to take an early retirement. So now they claimed our rural mid-Ohio as home while Chuck commuted into the city to work his remaining nine years at McDonnell-Douglas. They were a friendly couple; fit right into our little community.

The Thompsons have a nine-year-old son, Stevie, who is a member of my cub scout den. Stevie could be termed a change of life baby, conceived in Anna's later years. Anna may be twenty years my senior, but we got along just great and I loved spending time with her. She was also a close friend of my aunt. Chuck and Anna have a grown daughter who's married and lives in Dallas. They try to visit her during summer vacation, but I imagine it's hard on them being separated.

"Come on in and set a spell," invited Anna.

"Thanks. How're you today?" I asked as I took a comfortable chair in her country styled living room. Her home contained a blend of antiques and rustic pieces; a half-barrel table flanked each end of an inviting pair of buttery soft tan leather sofas while multi-colored cotton braided rugs warmed the pine hardwood flooring. Calico print curtains hung on the adjoining kitchen windows. I studied the large oil painting that hung above the stone fireplace mantle; its western scene depicted cowboys on horseback during a cattle drive with rich golden colors painting the churned earth and distant mountain peaks. It must remind Anna of the Texan life she left behind.

"What can I get you? You look tuckered out. Bet you walked around half of Meadowood today," commented Anna.

"Think I did." I laughed at her accurate assumption. "But the weather was so pleasant today, I really enjoyed the fresh air, so I didn't mind. I have your Avon that you ordered and a new book to browse, if you want."

"Swell. Hmm, good meeting the other night."

"Yes, it was. Carol just told me today that the chief has approved using the station for our drive too," I told Anna as I sipped a glass of lemonade.

"Oh, that's great," Anna took a large swallow of her drink before pausing and glancing toward Merry, "by the way, who were those older ladies sitting by themselves at Frannie's? Did you know them? My goodness, if they put their heads together any closer while they whispered away, they'da looked like the two-headed woman at the county fair. Just a pair of busy bodies only there for the tea and cookies, if you ask me."

I snorted in laughter, almost choked on my drink, as I listened to Anna's description and knew exactly who she was describing.

"Think they're both neighbors of Aunt Fran's. I heard them talking about seeing someone late at night who wasn't with his wife,"

I chuckled, "except I wondered what they were doing running around that late themselves."

"Don't that beat all! Some people just ain't happy unless they can gossip and spread dirt on somebody else. Wonder who they were talking about? Oh my God, now I'm doing it!" said Anna as she clapped a hand to her mouth.

"I tell myself it's normal curiosity, but I'm guilty too. Shameful, isn't it? One of these days something more interesting will happen in Meadowood besides a cake sale or a food drive, and then we won't have to turn into a pair of busy-bodies like those old ladies," I remarked.

"So, let's talk about the jamboree this weekend. Stevie is as nervous as a Mexican jumping bean. He can't wait. Do you need anything? You and Ted got the weekend planned and have all the gear?"

"I think so. At least I hope so. You know, I'm bound to forget something, but I keep my notepad in my purse and jot down stuff as I think of it. We'll all meet at Fox Run Park early Saturday morning. I've got a full day of activities planned with the scouts then Ted Williams will camp out with the boys Saturday night and on Sunday I'll join them as we march over to the Granger farm and explore the corn maze. Should be lots of fun," I stated.

"The Granger farm? I heard Fred was selling out."

"Not that I know of. Fred Granger has been creating his corn maze every Halloween for kids in the county to play in for the past ten

31

years or more. He only started charging admission last year to help cover his expenses. He's always been so kind and generous, especially with the small children. When his wife, Louise, was alive they used to hold fall harvest parties in their barn. Everyone came from miles around to bob for apples, take hayrides, or enjoy home baked pumpkin pie and cookies that Mrs. Granger made. It was such a joyous time. When Louise died from cancer a couple years ago, he stopped the parties. It was so sad; the entire town mourned her passing. That was before you and Chuck moved here. Things just haven't been the same since, but at least Fred still makes the corn maze," I commented.

"I had no idea. I hope the rumor is false about his farm," Anna said.

"You know, you're the second person who told me the Granger farm is being sold... how odd."

"Well, I checked the weather forecast for the weekend. Looks like it will be cool but not too cold; I worried over whether to make Stevie wear long-johns under his uniform. He'd turn beet red if he knew I told you that. At least there isn't supposed to be any rain, just overcast and a bit of fog," Anna said.

"Sounds like perfectly spooky Halloween weather. Ted plans to tell some ghost stories around the campfire; the boys will love it. Well, gosh Anna, I've got to be going. The boys will be home from school in a few minutes. See you on Saturday morning?"

"Yes, I'll drop off Stevie and a can of chips or treats for the troop," Anna said as she showed me to the door.

"Thanks, Anna. See you later," I said as I hurried down the walk and half trotted to get home before my boys.

With barely minutes to spare, I had a pot of spaghetti sauce simmering on the stove and water boiling for the pasta. I rushed to set the table, grabbed a loaf of garlic bread and quickly sliced it then tossed it into a basket. I snatched the phone to call Aunt Fran about the fire station just as the kitchen door crashed open and my two sons vaulted into the house. They jumped over Mittens, who lay sprawled across a spot of warm sunshine in the middle of the tiled floor. The cat twitched his tail in greeting and stretched contentedly but didn't bother to move out of the way.

I shook my head in amazement. "You're awfully trusting. But one of these days..." I told Mittens as I shook my finger at him.

Mittens replied, "Mroww," and licked his fur.

I listened as the phone stopped ringing and heard Aunt Fran's voice on the other end of the line.

"Hello?"

"Hey, it's Merry. Just wanted you to know that the chief will allow us to use the station, but you've got to speak with him about the arrangements."

"I'll stop over tomorrow on my lunch break from the shop. Betty can cover for me," Fran said.

"Good. I'd go down, but I'm tied up tomorrow helping Colleen with the kindergarten class; she needs a teacher's aide."

"Don't worry. I've got this covered. Call you later tomorrow."

"Great. Thanks Aunt Fran." I hung up and punched in Barb Williams' office number to try to catch her before she left for the day.

"Wythe Insurance, this is Barbara. Can I help you?"

"Hi Barb, it's Merry. Hey, just wanted to let you know that we can definitely use the fire station for the food drive so if you want to draft a flyer, go ahead. You've got the dates, right? Just add the station as the central collection point. I can meet with you on Friday afternoon, no, make that morning, if you want to run copies."

"Okay. I've already got a PowerPoint slide started, so I'll just plug in the info. We can run off a hundred copies in just a few minutes, so Friday morning will be fine. Can you pop in about nine-thirty or ten? I've got a meeting after lunch," Barbara told me.

"Sounds like a plan. Thanks for your help, Barb. See you Friday then." I hung up and checked off one more item on my to-do list. I nodded and mentally ran through my plans for the rest of the week as I stirred my sauce and added the spaghetti noodles to the boiling water.

Doug found me with a satisfied smile on my face as he entered the kitchen and went about his gun lock up ritual.

"What's with you? You look like the proverbial cat that swallowed the canary."

"Hmm? Nothing. Just had a good day and happy to have you home," I said as I kissed him hello and turned back to serve dinner.

"If you say so. Why do I have the feeling that you're brewing something in that pretty head of yours?" Doug asked.

Chapter 5

Screams and squeals of excited five and six-year-old kindergarten children filled the room as finger paint liberally smeared hands, faces and some clothing in Mrs. Klausson's classroom. A row of round pumpkins with colorful faces grinned back at me as I moved from child to child, cleaning paint from little hands and wiping runny noses. The morning had been spent in sheer bedlam, but the children were delighted with their pumpkin creations.

Mrs. Klausson clapped her hands and called for order in the classroom as the children obediently lined up in a row.

"Nice job, everyone. Time for our morning snack. Everybody find your seat. Mrs. Gardner will pass out milk and some special Halloween cookies," said the teacher.

"Hooray!" clapped the children as they eagerly received their treat and scattered about the room to claim a chair and table.

When I finished serving each child, I signaled to the teacher that I was stepping out to use the restroom. She nodded to me as she supervised the class and walked among the short, round table and chairs. I scooted out the door and hurried down the hallway toward the girl's bathroom to wash off my own remnants of water paint.

Joseph Cooper, the school custodian, pushed a wide dust mop across the hall's vinyl linoleum flooring. He smiled and stopped when he saw me.

"Gotcha good. Those little ones are a handful, aren't they?"

"Good morning, Mr. Cooper. Yes, they sure are, but they had so much fun. What's a bit of paint?" I held up both palms for his inspection. "My hands look pretty in red, blue, and yellow; don't you think?"

"You use a good squirt of that hand soap in there, ought to come right off," he suggested.

"That's just where I'm headed. How are you today, Mr. Cooper? How's that knee feeling in this cooler weather?"

"Not too bad. Nice of you to ask, Mrs. Gardner."

"Please, call me Merry. I've known you too long to stand on formality."

He nodded and said, "Best I get back to work before I get sacked."

"The school couldn't do without you, Mr. Cooper. You keep things in order around here," I assured him.

"Joseph Cooper is such a kind old gentleman," I reflected, as I entered the washroom to scrub away the finger paint. *"He always has a friendly smile and word for the children. Such a shame that a man in his seventies can't retire with security but is obligated to continue working to make ends meet."*

Mr. Cooper had been employed for thirty years by the Dickson Tire and Rubber plant in nearby Pottstown when the plant declared bankruptcy and closed its doors. He was lucky he could claim retirement, unlike others who were simply shown the gate. Unfortunately, the company slashed pensions by forty percent because of the bankruptcy, leaving their retired employees with only a portion

36

of their promised retirement income. People like Joseph Cooper had to find part-time jobs to make up for the loss of income and struggled to get by in today's economy. A sad story that was happening all too often.

Meadowood School was lucky to get him. His tall, gangly frame and balding head could be spotted sweeping floors or wiping up spills in the hallways and classrooms. The children knew that he always carried mint candies as a treat for them, tucked away in the pockets of his khaki colored work clothes, and clamored to gain his attention or hug him hello. In the mornings before the bell rang, he stood outside acting as crossing guard and assumed his sentry post in the afternoon when the dismissal bell sounded. The children loved him and so did the teachers.

As soon as the kindergarten class dismissed for the day at twelve-thirty, I jumped into my mini-van and drove downtown to run errands. I found a parking spot along the curb on Park Avenue, then checked my notebook and list of things to do before locking the van and heading out. First stop, the florist to pick up some pretty mums for a centerpiece. So many colors and types of mums were on display in the shop, my favorite fall flower. The spider mums tempted me with their unique shape, but I decided to opt for the traditional button variety. Finally choosing a color, I left the florist carrying a six-inch pot of fragrant yellow mums.

Next, I needed to pop into the butcher shop to buy a nice pork roast for Friday's dinner party. I crossed the street and walked toward

37

Sam's. As I approached, I saw Fred Granger standing in the doorway; he gestured wildly and shook a clenched fist. He appeared to be in a heated altercation with Sam Tilley, the owner of the butcher shop. Their loud voices carried on the wind, but I could make out snatches of conversation as I neared.

"You heard me!" Granger growled.

"Is that a threat? You'll be sorry."

"... the sheriff can decide..."

I watched as Fred stormed down the street and climbed into a battered pickup truck. The tires squealed as he sped away. Sam slammed the shop door shut just as I approached. I paused, wondering if I should go into the store or not. He must have seen me through the glass door, though, and beckoned me to come in.

"Ah, hello Sam. Open for business?" I asked, as I hesitated to step into the empty butcher shop.

"Of course."

"Everything okay?" I inquired.

"Yeah, sorry you witnessed that; it was nothing. Just a misunderstanding. What can I do for you?"

"Um, I was looking for a nice pork roast, enough to feed four adults."

Tilley, a scowl on his face, moved behind his counter and opened a glass refrigerator case, selecting a few cuts of meat and weighing each before he shared his choices.

"Got a nice four-pound crown roast that would work or maybe you'd prefer a boneless pork loin like this one. It's about three and a half pounds and would be easy to carve and feed four. I can give you a good price on the loin, if you like, say $3.49 per pound," the butcher offered. He gave me a take it or leave it look and waited for my answer.

"All right; I'll take the pork loin."

"Gimme a minute and I'll wrap it up for you," Tilley said.

I paid for the roast and left the shop but couldn't stop thinking about the argument I had witnessed. Fred Granger's face had mottled red with anger, caused by more than just a slight misunderstanding. As I opened my car door, I turned back to glance at the butcher shop and was surprised to see Sam hang a closed sign on the door then lock up. Seemed rather early to be closing business for the day. Grabbing my notebook, I scribbled down a few quick thoughts.

"Tilley is a strange character; very quiet, and stays to himself, odd for a merchant," I mused. I don't think I've ever seen him attend any town function, not even a Chamber of Commerce meeting. He opened the butcher shop about five years ago, but before that, no one knows where he came from or much else.

Friday morning, Barb Williams and I were busy printing off flyers and stacking them into piles of twenty-five each for distribution around town. They looked great. Barb had added some clip art with a Thanksgiving theme and centered the food donation information in a

39

bordered text box. The attractive notices should draw some attention when they were placed in storefront windows.

"Did you have to ask Ron permission to work on these flyers? I mean, using the printer and taking time away from your office duties," I said.

"No, he doesn't mind, especially since I'm helping you. It's for a good cause," Barb answered.

"Well, it's very nice of him. I'll be sure and thank him again when I see him at dinner."

"He mentioned that you had invited him to a dinner party. I think he's looking forward to spending the evening with Colleen," said Barb with a knowing laugh.

"I bet he is. He's bonkers for her. I just have to convince my friend to overlook his football leanings and see the man for himself. Colleen is so pretty with her Irish green eyes and auburn hair; she could have any man she wants. Sometimes I think she's playing hard to get with Ron; I've seen her considering him when she thinks no one is looking. Those two are a pair."

"Ron deserves someone special. He's a great boss; really knowledgeable about insurance and so considerate. Doesn't assign too heavy of a workload on me either."

"That's great. I bet your office must insure most of the homes and businesses around here," I said, waiting to ask what I actually wanted to know.

"Probably. Of course, some of the commercial properties are insured with agents located in Columbus," Barb answered.

"How about farms? Is the Granger farm insured with you guys?" I asked outright.

"Yes, that's one of Ron's accounts. Granger property is due for renewal next month. Why?"

"Oh, just wondering. I heard some rumors around town that the farm might be up for sale, like maybe his land would be used for development of a big mall. I was curious if your office had received any notice."

"No, this is the first I've heard that news. Can't imagine Fred Granger selling out; that farm has been in his family for generations," Barb speculated.

"That's what I thought too. Maybe it's just a false rumor," I said as I rubber-banded the flyers and placed them in a hefty tote bag. "Guess we're done. I better let you get back to work and I'll drop off some of these on my way home. Thanks for all your help."

"No problem. See you at the jamboree Saturday."

"Okay. Be sure and have Joey bring his scout project and dress warmly."

"Will do."

Chapter 6

S oft candlelight glowed and a fragrant autumn, cinnamon-like scent drifted across the room from the pair of Yankee Candle tumblers that I had lit. I stood back to admire my handiwork; I had draped our oak dining room table with a pale pumpkin colored tablecloth and arranged my best china dishes at each place setting. An amber cut-glass bowl held an assortment of white, yellow and bronze mums; I placed the lovely fall centerpiece on the table.

I glanced about our home, satisfied with the cool sage green colored sofa and matching draperies in the living room and the pair of light tan recliners. A side chair covered in a sage and tan tweed fabric coordinated with the other pieces. Our home wasn't fancy, but it was comfortable and serviceable with two young boys and one furry baby. I took a moment to admire the serene scene of the Thomas Kinkade painting that Doug and I had splurged on for our fifth anniversary. It hung above the fireplace and was flanked by a pair of my grandmother's antique brass candlesticks on the mantle.

The pork loin roasted in the oven while I added cheddar cheese to my casserole dish of au gratin potatoes. I checked the asparagus spears cooking on the stovetop then decided to add a bowl of applesauce sprinkled with a bit of cinnamon and sugar to the side dishes offered. I enjoyed fixing a special meal for guests; since most of our entertaining was usually limited to hotdogs or hamburgers with children. A more formal dinner was a pleasant change.

Doug came in and glanced at the clock.

"How much time do I have?" he asked as he put away his deputy gear then rushed upstairs to shower and change for dinner.

"About half an hour. I need you to play bartender tonight," I called after him. I think I heard a muffled okay as he closed the bathroom door.

Hair still damp, Doug strode into the kitchen wearing a pair of tan Dockers and an olive-green pullover sweater. He draped an arm about my shoulders and nuzzled me behind my ear. I inhaled the light masculine aftershave lotion that he wore.

"You look fabulous, Babe," he murmured.

"Not too much?" I asked. I spun about in a quick twirl; my crepe dress floated about my legs. I fingered the gold chain that lay against the dark blue fabric. I fluffed my short curls and tilted my head so he could view the matching earrings.

"Perfect. Table looks pretty too, hon, and dinner smells delicious. I see you're pulling out all the stops," Doug said.

"I just want dinner to be nice," I said as we shared a quick kiss.

"It's only Ron and Colleen. You don't have to try and impress them."

"I know."

43

When the doorbell rang a few minutes later, I found Ron and Colleen both waiting on the front steps. Ron had parked his car out front. I welcomed them both as I shot Colleen a questioning look.

"Did you two ride together?" I asked her.

"No. I walked. I'm only a block away; it's silly to take a car for such a short distance," Colleen answered.

"Come on in and make yourselves comfortable. Dinner will be ready in just a minute."

"Hey Doug, how's it going?" asked Ron Wythe.

"Same old stuff," said Doug, handing Ron a beer.

"By the way, Ron, I wanted to thank you for allowing Barb to help me with those flyers for the food drive. Kind of you to let us use that fancy color printer of yours," I told him.

"No problem. Anything for a good cause," Ron said, as his eyes shifted to Colleen.

"Everything looks fabulous. Can I help in the kitchen?" asked Colleen.

"Sure. If you could carry the vegetable dishes to the table, I'll get the roast carved."

"Colleen, what do you want to drink?" asked Doug as he poured a glass of white Zinfandel wine for me.

"I'll have the same as Merry, thanks."

"Okay folks, dinner's ready."

"The table looks lovely; so festive," commented Colleen.

"Well, I'll be eating off paper plates all weekend so I thought it would be nice to have a proper dinner for just once."

We passed around bowls and served the garlic-seasoned pork roast then we all turned our attention to the delicious hot food. I felt a furry head rub against my leg and heard a familiar meow as Mittens crawled under the table begging for handouts.

Ron reached down to pet the top of Mitten's head. "Hey boy, looking for some food?"

"Don't encourage him, he's got a bowlful in the kitchen. However, I suppose one little piece of meat will be okay," I told Ron as I watched him slip a piece of pork under the table.

Mittens purred his appreciation, "Mroww."

In between bites of her meal, Colleen described the upcoming Halloween party at the school.

"So, after the kids finish trick or treating around the neighborhood Wednesday night, they can join everyone in the school cafeteria for treats and games. Some younger children might feel safer attending the party. It can be rather scary facing all those costumes in the dark night."

"I think that's an excellent idea. I remember when my boys were toddlers and it frightened them confronting spooky faces and wild costumes. We usually only walked up and down one street just to give them some Halloween experience," I said.

45

"Have to admit, some of today's costumes can be pretty gruesome, like Freddie Krueger or Jason. Whatever happened to clowns and hobos?" asked Ron with a laugh.

"I know what you mean. Johnny told me he plans to be a zombie this year," I said, shaking my head.

"If you want an extra pair of hands to set up the school party, I'm available," offered Ron as he smiled at Colleen.

I caught Doug's attention as our eyes silently communicated. I smiled knowingly; cupid had nothing on me.

After we finished eating dinner, I set up coffee and cake on the coffee table in the living room where we could relax and enjoy our dessert.

Colleen helped to slice the spice cake with its buttercream frosting and served everyone a plate while I poured hot coffee.

"Mmm, this is superb, Merry," said Ron as he ate a bite of the dessert. "The entire dinner tasted delicious."

"Thanks. Glad you liked it."

"What time does the scout jamboree start tomorrow? It's all some of the boys in school can talk about," Colleen said.

"We've got a busy weekend planned. My den meets me at Fox Run park about nine o'clock on Saturday morning. We'll be hiking in the woods, maybe try some tracking, compete in games with the other dens, then camp overnight. Ted Williams has volunteered to take the overnight shift and on Sunday we explore the corn maze. Should be lots of fun for the boys," I said.

46

"Is that the Granger corn maze?" asked Colleen.

"Yes, it is. You know, Fred designs that maze every Halloween. The kids love it. It would be a shame if we lose that," I said, waiting to hear some reaction from Ron.

"Don't you think Fred will create one next year?" asked Ron, puzzled by my statement.

"Well... if that big mall is developed, I guess the land will be gone."

"What mall? The planning commission hasn't voted on any approval for a shopping mall," stated Ron emphatically.

"Are you sure? I've been hearing rumors all over town that Ted Williams plans to develop Fred Granger's farm for a big mall," I said.

"Well, I'm on the commission and I underwrite the farm's insurance policy so I would know if that was true, and I say it's not."

"Interesting. Guess those rumors must be false."

"Will you be at this scout thing?" Ron asked Doug.

"I'll be there for a few hours on Saturday. The Sheriff has assigned two deputies to patrol the jamboree grounds since there will be so many scouts from around the state joining our troop," Doug stated.

"Wow, how many kids will be at this thing?" asked Ron.

"I think the final count on registration was about a hundred and thirty," I said.

"That's a lot of kids."

"Sure is. I just hope we don't have any problems," said Doug.

Colleen and I chatted about school issues and the fall sweaters on display at Frannie's Frocks, while the guys turned to talk of football as

47

the evening wore on. It was a friendly, relaxed atmosphere as we shared each other's company. Finally, Colleen stood up and reached for her purse and coat.

"I've got to be going. I've got a ton of paperwork at home and semester plans to complete before Monday," Colleen said.

"Let me give you a ride home," offered Ron as he held her coat for her. "It's too late to walk alone."

Colleen hesitated for a second, raised an eyebrow at me, then smiled to Ron. "Thank you. That would be nice."

"Thanks again for a wonderful evening, Merry. Hey Doug, we need to get together for a tailgate party next week before the Buckeye's game."

"Yeah, let's do that," said Doug as he shook Ron's hand and we both saw our friends to the door. I watched as Ron held Colleen's hand as they walked to his car.

"Well, Mrs. Gardner, you hosted another successful dinner party and I see your matchmaking efforts have not been wasted," Doug complimented me with a quick hug and light kiss. "Let's get this stuff cleaned up; the night's still young."

I laughed and gave him, what I hoped, was my seductive smile, "What did you have in mind?"

Chapter 7

D oug placed the last box in the back of my van; loaded with tents and sleeping bags plus boxes of food stuffs. Billy and Johnny climbed into the rear seat and hooked their seat belts while I read my list and double checked that we had everything we'd need for the weekend.

"That it?" asked Doug.

"I think so." I adjusted my den mother scarf about the neck of my uniform and tightened the knot. I glanced back at the boys. "You guys both have on some thick socks with those boots? Got jackets and sweatshirts in your knapsack?"

"Yeah, Mom. We're good," replied Johnny.

"You didn't leave anything at Grandma's house last night, did you?" They both shook their heads to the negative. "Okay then. Guess we're off."

Doug waved to us as he climbed into his police cruiser and we pulled out of the driveway ahead of him.

Fox Run Park sat on a tract of fifty acres and was operated by the county. The densely wooded park contained a small lake well stocked with trout for fishing and several picnic groves with tables enjoyed by the community in warmer weather. The campground sites were normally full year-round and even offered restroom facilities throughout the sites. In winter the park trails were jam-packed with cross-country skiers and the local fishermen delighted in ice fishing on the lake when it froze solid.

Our drive to Fox Run Park was short, only fifteen minutes, and I pulled into one of the parking spaces in the graveled lot. I got out of the van and looked around for my group of scouts, recognizing a few of my parents' cars in the lot. I opened the hatch lid on the van, strapped on my backpack and started loading up Billy and Johnny with sleeping bags and tents. I grabbed our den flag and juggled it under my arm as I balanced two boxes of food stuffs.

"Hello!" shouted Anna Thompson as she and Stevie approached our van. "Need a hand? Stevie, help carry that flag for Mrs. Gardner."

"Thanks a bunch."

Joey Williams joined us with his father, Ted. Ted was equally loaded down with camping equipment. He smiled and nodded as he adjusted backpack shoulder straps. Bryan Goodwin arrived with Tommy Simon and his mother, Donna. Finally, I saw Martha Parker pull up with her son, Jerry.

"Hey everyone," greeted Martha. "I brought a box of oatmeal cookies."

"Oh yummy, thanks. I'm sure the boys will gobble them up plus we're going to make s'mores," I told her.

"We ready?" asked Ted as he marshalled the boys to form a line and march toward our campsite.

"Let's claim our site and get set up, including tents; we've got lots to do today," I directed as we headed into the wooded park.

I stuck our flagpole into the ground to mark our site; the blue pennant with our den number five fluttered proudly in the light breeze.

"If anyone needs to leave camp for bathroom usage or any other reason, find your way back by looking for our flag."

An hour later, we had pup tents erected and grouped together in a small circle. The boys scoured the area for large stones and added them to some bricks to create a protected campfire in the center of the circle. We tossed in small pieces of wood, stacked kindling and crisscrossed a few short logs on top. It would be ready to light when we returned from our hike. Finally, I placed the legs of a portable grill to rest across the perimeter of the circle, the mesh surface of the grill perched over the top of the woodpile.

"Okay boys gather round. We will start our hike in the park, and I want you Bears and Wolves to identify leaves for the trees you listed on your posters. A good scout is always aware of his surroundings. Team up and work together in pairs," I instructed.

Ted spoke up and explained what the older Webelo scouts would do, "We will practice our tracking skills today. As we hike, look for footprints in the soft dirt and mud, especially by the lake, and see what animals we can identify."

"Stay together with Mr. Williams or myself," I called out as I headed out with the younger boys.

"Let's take the trail on the right and head toward the lake," Ted said as he led his handful of Webelo scouts.

51

"What kind of animals do you think we'll find?" asked Joey.

"Probably rabbits, maybe a possum or two and definitely some deer. Remember what we read? Count the number of toes or claw marks in the footprint. Who remembers what kind of animal has four toes on their front and rear feet?" Ted inquired.

"Is that a rabbit?" answered Jerry Parker.

"Yes, that's right. Okay, how many toes does a possum have or how about a cat?"

"Um, a think a cat has four toes, but you don't see their claws 'cause they can hide them. Ain't that right, Mr. Williams," Stevie proudly explained.

"Correct. Now see here; everybody, kneel down. Careful now, don't step on it. What do you see?" asked Ted.

Excited, the boys all gathered around the indentation in the soft earth. They gently pressed fingertips into the print. Almost as one, you could hear them counting the dents in the ground from tiny toes.

"Five! I count five toes. That makes it a possum," declared Johnny.

"Now look at the size of the footprint. Do you think this is a large print or small?"

"Um, small," they all agreed.

"If it was larger, it might be a bear," reminded Ted.

"Whoa, are there bears in the woods?" asked Stevie.

"We do have some brown bears in Ohio, but probably not in this area. Don't worry. Let's move on. Keep your eyes on the trail; see if you can find any deer tracks."

I followed the path on the left toward the lake where we would join Ted and the other boys in our den. Billy, Tommy, Harold and Bryan shuffled their feet in the fallen leaves and tried to act excited when they found an oak leaf or a maple. I described the different trees with their leaves of bristled tips or rounded lobes and which colors belonged to which tree.

"Now I'm sure you all know what kind of leaf this identifies without my telling you. Please don't touch it. What kind of plant has three leaves and pointed edges?" I asked.

"Poison ivy," they all said in unison.

"Right. Be sure and watch for poison ivy and even poison sumac when you are hiking; it's no fun having an itchy rash. Okay, so what direction are we headed; north, west, east or south?"

I waited while the boys stood still, studied the trees and stared through the canopy of thick branches above their heads.

"I can't see the sun. How can we tell which way we're going?" cried Bryan.

"Look at the trunks of the trees near us. Do you see any moss? What side of the tree does moss grow on? Think about it."

"Oh, I get it. North. Moss grows on the northern side where it's shady. Here's some," exclaimed Billy.

53

"Very good. So, if this side of the tree is north, what compass point is opposite?"

"Um, south?" Tommy answered in a hesitant voice.

"Exactly. You boys are very smart. Now let's see if we can find some wild blackberries or maybe spot some crabapple trees," I said as we continued down our trail.

I could hear Ted and the boys crashing through the underbrush on their trail. They weren't practicing silent tracking methods, that's for sure, and likely scared away any small critters in the woods. I laughed to myself as we approached the banks of the lake and waited for the other half of our den.

"Okay, you guys, spread out and pick some of those blackberries we spotted in the brambles. Watch out for prickly branches. Here's a paper sack; put your berries in that."

Billy and Harold ran ahead of Bryan and Tommy as they whooped and laughed, their energy never ending. I smiled tolerantly as I watched them dash toward the sweet treasure.

I turned as I heard voices and spotted the rest of my den hiking toward the lake bank. Ted stood several paces behind them and was engaged in an animated conversation with Fred Granger. Their angry voices reached me; I was surprised to see Fred, although his farm and nearby corn maze bordered the park. Both men stood their ground and appeared unwilling to back down, and I wondered what they quarreled about. I stared as Fred Granger finally stomped off toward his own land, and Ted continued toward where I waited.

"What was that all about?" I asked him.

"Nothing much. Stubborn old coot," Ted fumed.

"Is this about that new shopping mall?"

"What? Don't know what you mean."

"Okay, if you say so. Hey, the boys are collecting some wild blackberries. They should be about done; let's gather them up and return to camp," I suggested.

"Sure," Ted agreed, and shouted to the boys to gather round.

We slowly marched back to our campsite, but my mind kept recalling the argument I had just witnessed and speculated again what was between Fred Granger and Ted. I couldn't help but feel Ted wasn't being truthful with me. I'll have to think about it later.

I delegated one of the older boys to place the berries in a large plastic container and rinse them with a couple bottles of clean water.

"Johnny, hand out some cold bottles of drinking water to everyone while Mr. Williams and I get the fire started. We'll cook some hotdogs for lunch," I said. I sorted through the box of food stuffs, pulling out bags of chips and rolls.

Once the fire burned hot enough, I arranged a pound of wieners across the grill and watched them sizzle, rolling them over occasionally. Everyone grabbed a paper plate, then like an assembly line, added a hotdog roll and a handful of chips. I doled out juicy char-grilled hotdogs to each scout as they moved down the line. We all sat Indian style around the circle as we wolfed down our lunch and listened to the descriptions of the animal signs that were tracked by the Webelos.

Our afternoon consisted of several competitions between our scout troop and other troops from neighboring counties. First, we tried our best at a tug-of-war contest, but our cub scouts are young and not very large, so they found themselves out-weighed and unfortunately were easily defeated. We had more luck with the three-legged race. Our scout's youth and spryness became an asset in that race, and we rejoiced with two out of three wins.

I laughed and cheered encouragement as our troop divided into two teams and tackled the obstacle course laid out with old tires, balance boards, and a thick climbing rope.

"Go Stevie, you can do it!" I shouted. "Come on Billy, hustle, hustle."

Hours later, I clapped and congratulated our champions as we trudged back to our campsite and some exhausted boys collapsed onto their pallets. They'd had a very busy day.

"You boys all wash hands and faces while I help prepare dinner, then we're going to roast marshmallows and make s'mores."

"Hooray," cried the scouts as they marched toward the park's community bath house and restrooms located about a hundred yards from our campsite.

Dinner was a quick meal of hamburgers, more potato chips, apple slices and cups of Gatorade. Dusk had fallen as we lit our battery-operated lanterns and placed them about the circle of tents. I apportioned all the ingredients for s'mores – large marshmallows, pieces of delicious Hershey chocolates, and squares of graham crackers.

Re-energized by their supper, the boys all sat around the campfire holding long slim branches they had scavenged earlier. Each speared a puffy marshmallow and thrust it into the flames to allow it to melt and blacken.

"Quick, pull your stick out, Bryan, before your marshmallow falls off," I directed. "Slide it onto your cracker; careful, that gooey stuff is really hot."

"Like this?" asked Bryan as he pressed the melted goo onto the cracker, added a piece of milk chocolate then topped it with a second graham cracker to create his sweet, oozing sandwich.

"Looks perfect to me," I said, as I handed more marshmallows to the other boys.

"Mmm, these are good, Mom," said Billy.

I noticed a circle of chocolate smeared around his mouth and some liberal smears on his shirt. I shook my head. *"Oh well. He'll need a good scrubbing in the tub when he gets home tomorrow,"* I thought.

"You okay for the rest of tonight?" I asked Ted. "I'll leave out the s'mores ingredients in case you get hungry later and here's the box of oatmeal cookies from Martha. That ought to hold them."

"Yeah, we'll be fine. Think we'll tell some ghost stories before bedtime. These guys will be on a sugar high for a while, but I think they're pretty tired, it'll be an early lights out," said Ted.

"You're right about the sugar high; hope they all settle down for you. I'm going to pack up and head home. See you after breakfast," I said.

I stood and stretched cramped muscles, then glanced around the camp and did a quick head count to make certain everyone was accounted for. "Okay guys, I will see you in the morning and we'll hike over to the corn maze."

"Who's ready for some spooky ghost stories?" Ted proposed as he doused one of the lanterns. Shadows increased in the flickering light of the campfire while a light fog began to roll in.

The boys giggled and I heard a collective "Ooh," as I grabbed my pack and walked toward the parking lot. I was looking forward to my own hot bath and soft bed.

Little did I know what the morning would hold.

Chapter 8

Yellow crime tape stretched across the entrance to the Granger farm and corn maze. I stared at the grim reminder of the tragic end to our scout jamboree yesterday. After three hours of sitting in the sheriff's office trying to recall every minute spent at the maze and park, I finally finished writing my report of our troop's activities, then drove back to the farm to retrieve my forgotten backpack, left behind where I had dropped it in all the excitement.

I now knew that Fred Granger was the murdered man. Why would anyone want to hurt him? He lived alone and farmed his land. His daughter had married and moved away, but I think I recalled that he had a son who lived somewhere in the state. Heaven knows what will become of his farm now. Maybe it would turn into that shopping mall after all. Hmm...

I found my backpack lying in the dirt among some broken corn stalks. I picked it up and brushed off loose soil and leaves. I gazed at the entrance to the corn maze, drawn to it. Ducking under the yellow crime tape, I crawled into the corn labyrinth. I plodded the path, moving toward the spot where we had found the body. Scattered debris across the path marked the way forward like Hansel and Gretel's breadcrumbs. Broken stems and leaves, torn wrappers from bandages gave evidence of medical personnel that had crowded into the narrow space.

I continued my exploration of the maze; the silence eerily deafening, only broken by the sound of the wind moving among the dried, brittle shoots. A pool of dark blood stained the earth. My shaky legs gave way as I slid down into a sitting position and stared at the spot where a man's life had ended. A shaft of sunlight pierced the thick growth and glinted on something metal buried under the leaves. I crawled on hands and knees and pushed aside the broken foliage until my hands touched two smooth metal objects. Pulling them out of the dirt, I turned one over in my hand to examine it. I recognized it immediately; it was a scout leader's neckerchief slide. Was it Ted's?

My hand clutched the other object; I slowly opened my fist and gawked at the oddly shaped key. Whose was it? Did Fred drop it? What did it open?

Unzipping a pocket of my backpack, I tossed in both key and slide as goosebumps danced along my forearms and the back of my neck tingled. I needed to get out of this spooky place and fast. Without a backward glance, I rapidly traced the maze path back to its entrance and ran to my car.

I tossed my bag into the back seat, climbed into my van and started back toward home. I'd had enough of the maze. As I drove past Frannie's Frocks, Aunt Fran waved me down and motioned for me to stop. I found a place to park along the curb and went into her shop.

"Oh, my goodness, I just heard about Fred!" exclaimed my aunt.

"Are you and the boys okay? You were there with the scouts, weren't you?"

"We were there all right; poor Billy stumbled upon the body and let out a blood-curdling scream. Scared the living daylights out of me, I don't mind telling you."

"Oh, the poor child. Where is he now? What about Johnny?"

"I left both of the boys with my mom and dad. I told them they could stay home from school. You know mom, she'll spoil them rotten and load them up on sweets to aid their recovery," I replied.

Aunt Fran chuckled, "Yes, I can just picture my sister doing that. Well, the important thing is that you're all safe. What did Doug say about the murder?"

"I haven't had an opportunity to talk with him yet; I spent most of the morning at the station."

"Do you think it was an accident?"

"Unless Fred Granger tripped, fell, and bashed his head on a shovel several times. No, it was not an accident," I said, as the scene flashed through my mind again.

"Oh, dear."

"Can I talk to you later, Aunt Fran? I'm beat and just need to get home."

"Of course. I'm sorry. You take care." Aunt Fran enveloped me in a quick hug and kissed me on the cheek.

"I'll call you if I hear anything and you do the same," I said as I left the shop.

Mittens greeted me at the door; he meowed and rubbed his head against my leg. I gave him a quick knuckle rub on his head, then turned on my tea kettle. All I wanted now was a nice cup of hot tea and a soft chair where I could put my feet up and relax.

As soon as I reclined in Doug's chair, Mittens hopped up onto my lap. He butted his head against my arm and patted my cheek with his paw. His feline affection and concern touched me.

"Thanks, boy. I needed that." I laid my head back and closed my eyes. Mittens' purring grew louder; his little engine vibrating as he cuddled against me.

Thirty minutes later, I awoke to the sound of the telephone ringing. Mittens jumped off my lap as I stood and grabbed for my cell phone laying on the kitchen counter.

"Hello," I said as I glanced at the caller I.D.

Colleen's voice rose an octave, her words rushed as she babbled on the other end of the line, "Oh my God, are you okay? I just heard about the murder. I can't believe it. Fred Granger of all people; who would want to kill him?"

"Slow down. We're all right, but I've been asking myself the same question. Who would hurt poor Fred? It makes no sense."

"Do you need anything? I feel like I should do something to help, but I don't know what. Do you think I should hold the Halloween party at the school? Some of my teachers are wondering if parents will allow their children to participate in Halloween this year. What do you think?"

"I haven't even thought about Halloween. Actually, having the party at school might be the safest solution for the kids; keep them off the streets. Don't cancel that," I said. The idea of a murderer walking around our town just sank in.

"You're right, you're right. How can you be so composed when you were right there and I'm running around like a chicken with my head cut off?" Colleen asked. She took a deep breath as she tried to sound normal.

"I think I'm still numb. This is not being calm, believe me," I laughed.

"Okay, call me if you need me. I gotta go."

"Bye. Talk with you later," I said, ending the call.

Colleen's expressed worries began to take root as I stared at my silent phone. I stood there for several minutes, thoughts swirling through my mind. The sound of the kitchen door shutting finally jarred me from my reverie.

Doug ushered Billy and Johnny into the house. He wrapped me into a bear hug, then studied my face.

"How you doin'?" Doug asked.

"I'm okay. I had a short nap and just talked to Colleen. She's worried about the Halloween celebration at school. You guys hungry?" I asked as I glanced between the three of them.

"How about a pizza tonight? You don't need to cook," Doug suggested.

Both of the boys heard pizza and shouted their approval.

63

"I'm so glad to have you all home. Come here and give your mother a big hug."

Billy and Johnny complied reluctantly. "Aww, Mom. We're not babies anymore."

"I know, but I needed that hug." I turned to Doug as the boys scampered into the living room and turned on the television. "Any news? What's going on?"

"The Sheriff is questioning Ted Williams. How'd he get blood all over him? Doesn't look good."

"Surely, Ted can't be a suspect. Ted was with the troop all night and with me Sunday morning. We don't even know when Fred was actually killed," I reasoned.

Johnny approached us with a worried look on his face. "Um, Mom? That's not right."

"What's not right, Johnny? What's the matter?" Doug asked.

"Well, um, I don't wanna get Mr. Williams in trouble or nothing, but he left the camp Saturday night."

"What do you mean, he left? After I went home on Saturday? He left you boys alone in the park at night?" I fumed.

"You know how Billy always has to get up and pee in the middle of the night? Well, he was afraid to walk down that dark path to the bathrooms by himself, so he woke me up. I peeked into Mr. Williams' tent and it was empty. I shined my flashlight into it and everything, but he wasn't there. I thought maybe he might be in the bathroom too, but we didn't see anyone else."

"You sure about that?" asked Doug.

"Yeah. I tried to stay awake awhile after we got back to our tents, but I guess I fell asleep. He was there in the morning," explained Johnny.

"Thank you, son. You did the right thing by telling us."

"I'm sure Ted can explain. There's got to be a reason he left camp and we don't really know how long he was gone. Maybe he just went back to his car to get something," I suggested.

"I need to let Sheriff Simmons know about this," said Doug.

"But Doug, think about it. Why would Ted possibly hurt Fred Granger? What motive could he have?" As soon as the words were out of my mouth, the memory of Ted and Granger arguing flashed across my mind.

Doug saw my expression and read the worried look that came into my eyes. "You know something. Don't you?"

Now it was my turn to stammer and hesitate. "Oh dear, I witnessed Ted Williams in a heated argument with Fred Granger on Saturday morning when we were hiking. He said it was nothing."

"Uh huh. One more reason he's moving to the top of our list. You and the boys eat without me; here's money for the pizza. I've got to get back to the station," said Doug as he pressed a kiss to my cheek and hurried out the door.

I stood staring at the closed door, my mind swirling with questions.

Chapter 9

"Mom, can we still go to the pumpkin farm and pick out our Halloween pumpkins? You promised," said Billy as he and Johnny got ready for school the next morning.

"How are you feeling today, Billy?"

"I'm okay."

"Are you sure? Do you want to tell me about that bad dream?" I asked as I smoothed his ruffled hair and pushed a lock out of his eyes. I caressed his cheek, the skin so soft and still baby-like, as I studied his face.

"No. Um, I don't wanna talk about it."

"How about the pumpkins, Mom. Can we go?" asked Johnny again as he strapped on his backpack.

With all that had happened, it had completely slipped my mind. Both of the boys looked at me expectantly. How could I say no? I gave them each a quick hug.

"Of course, we can. How about after school today? Come straight home so we can go and get back before dinner."

"Super! Bye Mom," waved Johnny as they ran to catch the school bus.

"Meow," Mittens reminded me he still needed to be fed as he rubbed his head against my shins.

"Okay, come on. I didn't forget you; you know. You need to learn some patience," I told the cat.

I tossed a load of laundry into the washing machine and turned it on before I gathered up a few Avon orders that needed delivery and headed out of the house. I drove over to Carol Goodwin's house to drop off her nail polish.

"Hi Merry," welcomed Carol as I stepped into her kitchen.

"Hi. How's Tommy doing?" I asked as I set the small Avon bag on the table.

"He's okay. I'm glad he didn't see the body, but it still upset him to know someone had died."

"Definitely was not what we had planned for the scout jamboree. I just keep thinking of poor Mr. Granger laying there."

"Does the sheriff have any idea yet who killed him?" asked Carol.

"I don't know. Doug hasn't told me anything and he's been in the office until late at night."

"Kinda creepy thinking about a murderer possibly living in our town."

"I know what you mean. Well you take care, I've got to be going," I said and headed to my next delivery.

I parked near Frannie's Frocks and walked the half block to the store. Bundled cornstalks wrapped with colorful orange yarn stood grouped with pots of bright yellow mums and various sizes of pumpkins to create a picturesque autumn display in front of the dress shop. Pulling open the glass door with its stenciled name, I stepped into the familiar shop with its racks of corduroy slacks and knit pullover tops, long-sleeve dresses and woolen plaid scarves. A square table held neatly arranged gloves in colorful wool and soft leathers. I spied Anna Thompson chatting with Aunt Fran as they examined a pile of new fall sweaters. They both looked up and smiled as I walked over to the front register.

"I've got those bath products that you ordered, Aunt Fran," I told her as I placed her purchase behind the counter.

"Great. I've been looking forward to trying those lavender bath salts," said Aunt Fran.

"Any news on the investigation?" asked Anna.

"Haven't heard anything, but you know how close-lipped Doug can be. He's ..."

Barbara Williams burst through the door, startling all of us. Her expression stopped me in mid-sentence.

"I saw your car out front," Barb cried.

"What's wrong?" I questioned and reached for her hand.

"The sheriff has arrested Ted!"

"What?! When?"

"Just now. Maybe a half hour ago. Ted didn't do it; he couldn't have," declared Barbara.

"Of course, he didn't," I agreed, but then I thought of all the questions that had been spinning around in my head since Sunday. Where was Ted Saturday night? What was the quarrel about that I had witnessed between him and Fred Granger?

"Can you do something, Merry? Can you speak with Doug?" asked Barb.

"I'm sure Sheriff Simmons knows what he's doing. I'll talk to Doug, but he's only a deputy and I don't know how much he can tell me."

"Ted's a good guy. He didn't do this," said Anna. "Can't you kind of check into things, sort of ask around? You know most everyone in town; I bet you can figure out who killed Fred."

"Whoa, I like Ted too and he's been a super scout leader, but I don't really know what I can do. You're giving me way too much credit. I'd like to help, really, but I just don't know what good I'd be." I looked at the three women; their faces all told a different story. Anna's expression was one of expectation, Aunt Fran appeared worried, and Barb's face veered between hope and fear.

"Please! Merry, you've got to try. I don't trust Simmons to look for another suspect if he has Ted locked up," Barb pleaded.

"We'll help," declared Anna.

"I wouldn't even know where to begin," I stammered.

"Then you'll do it? You'll help?" asked Barb again, wringing her hands and studying my face.

"Why do you even care?" asked Aunt Fran. "I thought you two divorced."

"Um, well, for Joey's sake and, um, I've always hoped that we could get back together," admitted Barbara.

I raised my eyebrow at that bit of news but said nothing. The idea of asking questions or interfering in police business is bound to get me in hot water with my husband, but Ted Williams is a good friend and I just can't stand by and do nothing. I sighed as I nodded, and Barb engulfed me in a tearful hug.

"Thank you. You're such a good friend. I knew I could count on you."

"I haven't done anything yet, but you have to promise me you'll accept whatever facts turn up about Ted," I warned her.

"Of course, but I just know he's innocent," said Barbara. She turned and hurried out of the shop, leaving the three of us behind and me wondering what I had just gotten myself into.

"Doug will be furious with me if I start snooping around and interfering with his case," I whispered as the enormity of what I had just committed to engulfed me.

"Do you think she's right? Is Ted innocent?" asked Aunt Fran.

"There are an awful lot of questions he needs to answer. I saw him arguing with Fred Granger on Saturday morning, and where did he go later that night? My boys told me he left the campground and I have no idea how long he was gone. I'm worried."

"Oh my, it doesn't look good for him. I had no idea," Anna drawled. "But, sugar, I just know you'll think of something and can figure it out." She smiled widely and linked her arm with mine in a conspiratorial manner.

70

"I think you need to find out where your scout leader took off to on Saturday night. That's the place to start," Aunt Fran speculated.

We broke apart as the bell jingled on the shop's door and a pair of customers walked in. I glanced at the clock and grabbed my purse as I prepared to leave.

"Call me later," whispered Aunt Fran as she approached her new customers.

I left the dress shop and hurried down the street to Martha's Bakery with no actual plan in mind and a hundred thoughts swirling through my head. Delicious aromas of cinnamon sticky buns and warm bread filled my senses as soon as I entered the store. Martha worked behind the clear glass display cases arranging plates of apple and bran muffins. She glanced up as I approached.

"Hello, Merry. What can I get you today?"

"Hi Martha. Um, do you have any more of those oatmeal raisin cookies that you brought to the jamboree?" I asked as I peeked into the display cases.

"Sure do. How many would you like?"

"Ah, how about three dozen? Would you put one dozen in a separate bag for me? I'm giving them to someone."

"No problem. Just take me a minute," said Martha.

"How's Jerry doing?" I asked.

"Oh, he's fine. By the way, thanks for protecting the boys and getting them safely away from that mess on Sunday. That was quick thinking on your part, and I appreciate it. I'm sure the other mothers feel that way too."

"Thanks. My only concern was for the boys," I said as I reached for the two bags and paid her.

"Enjoy the cookies," said Martha as she waved goodbye to me.

I quickly returned to my minivan, tossed my purse onto the floor, and laid the bags of cookies on the passenger seat. Pulling away from the curb, I headed for the sheriff's office on the opposite end of town. With any luck, I'd find my husband on duty inside.

The brick front building filled the corner lot of Broad Street and Park with wide parking lots to its left side and rear, empty save for a few parked, police cruisers. A carved wooden sign announced Meadowood Sheriff Office above the double set of glass doors. I hesitated a moment and took a deep breath before pulling open the door and entering the cool interior. I recognized the young deputy on desk duty as Tony Dalton and decided to take advantage of it.

The besotted deputy looked up at me with puppy dog eyes as I approached his desk. "Ah, um, hello Mrs. Gardner," he said with a timid smile.

"Hello Tony. Please call me Meredith. How are you today? Is my husband in the office?" I asked sweetly. Mother always told me you could catch more flies with honey than vinegar.

The shy deputy appeared flustered as he studied a sheet of paper on the desktop, then tried to answer me in a voice that squeaked. He cleared his throat and tried again in a lower tone, "Yes ma'am, he's in the back. If you'll wait just a minute, I'll ring his phone and let him know that you're here."

"Thank you, Tony. Would you like a cookie to eat with your coffee?" I offered as I handed him the open bag.

"Mmm, these look good. Thanks."

"No problem. You go ahead and enjoy that."

I waited a few minutes more until Doug pushed open the inner door and ushered me into the secured offices. His desk sat near a side window; a shaft of sunlight filtered through the blinds and shone on the dust motes floating in the air above a corner of the cluttered, gray utility desk.

"To what do I owe the pleasure of your visit?" Doug asked suspiciously. "Couldn't be because you heard we're holding Ted Williams for questioning, is it?"

"I haven't seen you since last night, that's all. I missed you. See, I brought you and the guys some cookies as a treat. Want one?" I placed the bag of cookies on his desk.

"I know that look, Merry. You're up to something."

"I am not. I was just wondering, though, if I could maybe say hello to Ted. You said he's only being questioned, not officially arrested, right? As his scout leader, I think it is my duty to ask him why he left the boys alone on Saturday. Can't I at least ask him one question?" I wheedled as I glided my hand up and down my husband's arm and batted my eyelashes. I waited expectantly.

73

"Hmm, you can stop that now. It's working." Doug firmly removed my hand and sighed defeatedly. "Five minutes. I'll let you speak with him for five minutes and that's it," conceded Doug.

"Thank you, dear. I promise, I'll just be five minutes."

"I could get in trouble for this and just when the sheriff appointed me to run point on this investigation. Don't let Simmons see you."

"I won't." I gave him a quick peck on the cheek as he led me toward the holding cells.

Ted Williams sat on the edge of a narrow cot, bent forward with his hands clutched between his knees. His stricken face held blank eyes that stared hopelessly. At the sound of my footsteps, he jerked upright.

"Merry! You've got to help me. Tell them I couldn't do this," he pleaded.

"Calm down, Williams. You've got five minutes," commanded Doug as he motioned Ted to step back, then unlocked the cell door. He opened the iron gate wide enough for me to step inside; I jumped as it clanged shut behind me.

"Hello, Ted." I glanced about the small confines, then perched on the only chair in the space. "I need to ask you where you went on Saturday night. My boys told me they saw your tent empty. What were you doing?"

"I can't answer that; someone else is involved."

"How long were you gone? Didn't you worry about leaving those children alone?" I hissed, angry now, I tried to keep my voice level.

"I'm sorry, Merry. I was only gone an hour. They were all asleep; nothing happened."

"They were not all asleep or Billy and Johnny would not have witnessed your absence. Anything could have happened. What if the campfire sparked or got out of control? I'm really disappointed in you, Ted."

"Guess I didn't think of that. I swear I wouldn't do anything to harm those kids and I most certainly did not kill Fred Granger. If I tell you something, will you keep it in confidence?" asked Ted.

"I can try, but not if it could help solve the murder."

"I met someone. She drove to the park and we got together in her car in the parking lot. I was never far away from the campsite."

"Will she vouch for you if the police ask?" I inquired, watching him closely.

"I can't ask her. She's married. We've been seeing each for the past month. Mostly I drive over to Pottstown and we get together at night while her husband works third shift at Paulson Chemicals. I won't tell you more than that."

"Remember when I saw you fighting with Fred Granger in the park? What was that about? The truth," I demanded.

Ted nervously glanced about the cell then back at me before he admitted grudgingly, "I wanted him to sell me a parcel of his land. He refused. He kept saying he wouldn't destroy the environment."

75

"You need to tell Doug or the sheriff everything you've told me. Don't you realize how guilty you look? If you didn't kill him, who did?"

"I'm in a hell of a mess, Merry. Please help me," cried Ted as he covered his face with his hands and leaned back against the wall.

I glanced at him worriedly and nodded as Doug returned and unlocked the door, then motioned me out of the cell. The gate clanged ominously.

Doug walked me to the outer door. He paused and placed a hand over mine as I reached for the door handle. "We need to talk later at home. I need to know what he told you, understand?"

"But Doug, it was in confidence. I promised him."

"You aren't his lawyer or his priest, Merry. There's no oath of confidentiality at risk here. We'll discuss this later."

"Okay," I agreed reluctantly then left.

Chapter 10

D ried leaves fluttered to the ground, only to be picked up by the brisk autumn breeze to scatter again into the air. I pulled on a pair of fleece gloves and pulled my jacket zipper up higher against the cool air.

We walked between rows of orange pumpkins nestled among thick pungent vines, hunting for the perfect Halloween jack-o'-lantern. Several people dragged little red wagons or carts across the furrows in search of the ideal size and shape pumpkin. There were small yellow ones the size of grapefruits and others so large it required two people to lift them. Clumps of dirt clung to the smooth winter squash as its deep orange skin shouted Halloween.

"You can each get one pumpkin. Try to find some nice medium ones," I shouted to Billy and Johnny as they ran from row to row on the pumpkin farm. Ross Pumpkin Farm and Orchard produced the largest crop of squash and pumpkins in the county and allowed the public to pick bushels of sweet apples from its orchard. The Ross family had farmed the land for over fifty years and delighted kids from all around with their hayrides and scarecrow decorations. Their farm was always a Halloween destination for the locals, and we traditionally made it one of our stops each October.

As I waited on the boys to make their selections, I browsed inside the enclosed produce stand and picked up a mason jar of homemade apple butter. There were cartons of fresh brown eggs, gourds of all shapes and golden squash, late corn on the cob, bunches of fragrant scallions, russet potatoes and bushels of apples for sale. I was weighing a bag of honey crisp apples when I spied the butcher, Sam Tilley enter the shelter.

"Hello," I greeted him as I walked over to where he was sorting through the ears of corn. "Can I talk to you for a minute?"

Sam shot me a quizzical glare then nodded his head, "I suppose so. Didn't I sell you a pork loin recently? Anything wrong with it?" he inquired defensively.

"Oh no, it was fine. I was just wondering if you'd tell me what you and Fred Granger had been fighting about when I came into the store last week? Looked serious to me."

"That's none of your business, lady. I don't have to answer your nosy questions. Now if you don't mind..." he growled as he pushed past me and slapped a few dollars down on the cashier's counter as he left with his bag of corn.

Well, well... wonder why he's so testy. I do believe Mr. Tilley is hiding something," I murmured to myself and jotted a note in my book.

Billy and Johnny rushed up to me; each proudly presenting their pumpkin choices to me.

"Mine is better than Johnny's. Isn't it, Mom?" declared Billy.

"Both look like excellent pumpkins for carving or painting. You need to think about what you want to do. If you paint the face, it will last longer, but if you carve it, you can place a lit candle inside," I said as we carried our purchases to the Ross' youngest daughter, Emily, waiting by the cash register.

Emily smiled shyly at Johnny and I noticed he started shuffling his feet from side to side and stammered a hello to her, then glanced away.

"Ah, puppy love," I thought and smiled to myself, watching my eldest become tongue-tied in front of the pretty girl. I'll have to watch what develops here.

"Come on boys, let's get home. You can design your pumpkins while I start dinner and later, we'll work on those Halloween costumes," I said. I placed the pumpkins, apples and my other finds into the back of the van then headed home as my mind replayed my conversation with Sam Tilley. I need to remember to share my observations with Doug.

Newspapers covered the top of the picnic table to catch the debris as Billy and Johnny carved and painted their Halloween pumpkins. Johnny carefully scooped out the seeds and guts from inside his pumpkin; the top lid had been cut and removed, then set aside. His boy scout pen knife slid into the pulp as he carved slanted eye sockets and pointed teeth. Billy applied brush and acrylic paint to his pumpkin as he channeled his inner artist and drew a sneering face. He would have less clean up afterwards and that was what mattered to him.

79

I watched the boys outside from my kitchen window as I prepared our evening meal. I saw Billy ask for Johnny's help once and, like the big brother that he was, he stopped his own project to assist. His action made me smile in approval and brought a tear to my eye.

"Hey there, are you crying? Everything okay?" asked Doug as he wrapped his arms about my waist and pressed a kiss against my hair.

"Just fine. I was just thinking how lucky I am to have such wonderful sons. Look at them. The boys are creating their Halloween pumpkins and helping each other. It's so sweet."

"They've got a good mama," said Doug as he gave me another affectionate squeeze. "Did you get those pumpkins from Ross's farm?"

"Yeah, we did."

"Sorry I couldn't get away to go with you."

"That's okay. Um, I saw Sam Tilley out there too; such a nasty man. He was really short tempered with me. All I did was to ask him why he was quarreling with Fred Granger last week and he practically snarled."

"What quarrel? What do you know of Fred and Sam fighting?" asked Doug as he stepped back to study my face, suspicion and worry in his eyes.

"Remember? I stopped at the butchers to buy that pork roast we ate for dinner last Friday. Fred and Sam were having a very heated argument on the sidewalk as I approached the store. Fred Granger literally stormed off and Sam slammed the door shut. I was afraid to

80

go in. I only heard snatches of it, but they were both red-faced and furious."

"Hmm... that's interesting. I heard Fred also had words with the bank manager on Friday. Seems like Fred had disagreements with several people around town. Maybe I better have a word with Mister Tilley," Doug said, a thoughtful expression on his face as he considered this recent information.

"What do we really know about Tilley? He never joins any of our community events. I know some people are just more private and stay to themselves and all, but he carries it to a whole extra level. The guy's a mystery. Gives me the creeps," I admitted to my husband as I carried plates to the table.

"Just because someone is quiet, does not make them a criminal. The man's just not a mixer, but I do plan to ask him about that confrontation."

"You do that. Poor Ted Williams is being held for something that I know he didn't do while there are plenty of other suspects around town. It's not fair," I cried, wringing my hands.

"If Ted's innocent, he'll be fine. The truth will come out."

"What are you going to do about his mystery woman that I told you about? Doesn't that give him an alibi for Saturday night?" I asked, chewing on my lower lip.

"The sheriff will look into it. Saturday night is really not our biggest concern now; the medical examiner put the time of death about thirty minutes, more or less, before your scouts entered that maze on Sunday.”

“Oh, my goodness! Then the murderer could have been there at the same time as us. Holy cow, that really scares me. By the way, did Ted tell you how he got that blood on his shirt?”

“Yeah, I shouldn’t be telling you this, but he claims he found Granger and tried giving him CPR, like the good little scout leader that he is.” Doug snorted, voicing his doubts of that statement.

“Don’t you believe him? I tried to find a pulse on the body, but when I pressed my fingers against the neck, there wasn’t any. So much blood everywhere. I couldn’t look at the poor man’s face; he was lying on his belly,” I told Doug as I envisioned the scene again.

“Are you sure? How does someone provide CPR to a body lying face down? A bit difficult to reach the chest and heart, wouldn’t you say?”

“Well, maybe Ted rolled him over. There’s got to be a logical answer,” I insisted.

“If there is, our department will find it. I hope you’re not getting involved in all of this.”

“Um, Ted asked for my help, so did Barb. I sort of promised,” I whispered and waited for his reaction. I didn’t have to wait long.

“Meredith Gardner, you stay out of this investigation. Sheriff Simmons will have my job if he catches you. This is dangerous business. Do I make myself clear?” Doug warned, in the stern voice he used when disciplining the boys.

"Yes, dear," I murmured with my fingers crossed behind my back.

"Mroww", Mittens looked up at me and butted my leg with his head as if to say that he wasn't fooled by my placid agreement.

Chapter 11

"Hello, Aunt Fran? Do you have any free time tonight? I was wondering if you could help me with Billy's Halloween costume; you sew much better than I do. He wants to be a spaceman, and I was thinking of that remnant piece of silver lamé fabric you showed me last month. Could I use that for his costume?"

"You mean like that old TV show, *My Favorite Martian*?"

"Huh? I don't think I know that one," I said perplexed.

"Sorry, before your time, I guess. But I get the general idea. Hmm, we could use long metallic pipe cleaners as antennae and sew the costume as a one-piece jumpsuit. That should work," suggested Aunt Fran.

"Sounds great. He might be able to wear Doug's motorcycle helmet too; it has a tinted face shield, just like astronauts. We could attach the antennae to that, or I could wrap them onto a plastic head band and have him wear them that way."

"Stop over about seven and I'll ask Anna to come too. Between the three of us, we should be able to knock out a costume in a few hours," Aunt Fran stated.

"Perfect. Thanks a bunch. I've got a pattern that will help too."

"See you later then," Aunt Fran said.

I hung up the phone and grabbed Billy as he reached for a cookie from the jar.

"Hold on, young man. I need some measurements from you if I'm to put together a space suit. Just stand there while I grab my tape measure."

"Aw Mom, can you hurry up? I'm missing Scooby-Doo."

"This will only take a minute. Now stand still," I said as I held my tape measure at the nape of his neck and dropped it down to see the overall length of the jumpsuit. I measured his arm length, then the inseam of his leg. Mittens decided to swat at the dangling end of the tape as it hung from my hand. He was having great fun as he leapt onto it and tried to capture the cloth snake.

"Mittens! You're not helping here," I laughed as I jotted down the measurements and pulled up my tape. "Sorry pal, find something else to attack."

"Mroww," Mittens growled as he sauntered away, his bushy tail pointed straight up with the tip curled over.

"Can I go now?" asked Billy.

"Yes, go ahead. I'll need you to try on the costume tomorrow and see how it fits. I can make adjustments if need be."

"Thanks, Mom. You're the best," Billy said as he gave me a quick, unexpected hug before running into the living room.

I smiled, then gathered up my sewing kit, pattern and supplies to take to Aunt Fran's house.

Doug looked up from his newspaper as I slung my purse strap over my shoulder and jostled my sewing kit in one hand and the bag of notions in my other.

85

"I'll be back late. Aunt Fran and I are working on Billy's Halloween costume. It'll probably take us several hours to finish."

"Be careful. Gimme a call if you'll be out past eleven," Doug said as he turned his attention back to the editorial page.

The porch light glowed a warm welcome as I approached my aunt's front door. I heard soft voices inside as I knocked once and twisted the doorknob to enter the cozy home.

"Aunt Fran... it's me," I called out as I closed the door behind me. I recognized Anna Thompson's short laugh and my aunt's voice coming from the kitchen, so I followed the sound.

"Hi, Merry," greeted Anna as I entered the brightly lit kitchen with its crisp white walls and slate blue counters above creamy white cabinets. Decorative blue and white delft china plates hung on one wall and a blue gingham swag valance draped the top of the wide kitchen window. My aunt's portable Singer sewing machine occupied one end of the cleared off table.

"I really appreciate both of you helping me like this. I hadn't planned on making a fuss with a costume this year for Billy, but he wanted something special to wear and I just couldn't say no. The poor kid is still having nightmares about seeing Fred Granger's body. I'm hoping Halloween will cheer him up," I explained.

"Oh dear, I'm sorry to hear he's having problems. Did you tell Doctor Stone about his dreams? Are they keeping Billy awake at night?" asked Aunt Fran.

"I haven't spoken to him, but I may have to. I sat up with Billy last night for two hours before I could get him back to sleep. He cries out in his sleep and twice now he's wet the bed. He hasn't had any issues with bed wetting since he was a toddler," I said.

"Well, let's see what you've got there," Anna said as she pulled the tissue pattern from its envelope and read over the directions.

"We need to make it roomy enough for a jacket or sweater underneath in case it's cold on Friday," suggested Aunt Fran.

"Good idea, although I'm not sure how long he'll really be out trick or treating. We may just do the school party and call it a night," I said. "Though, if we make it big enough, he could wear it again next year."

Anna voiced her concerns as she laid out the fabric and began pinning on pattern pieces, "Quite a few parents are afraid to let the kids roam the streets this year, what with having a murderer at large. We may limit Stevie's trick or treating too."

"I don't blame them. I'll probably escort my boys for a couple of blocks, then head over to the school."

"Is the Sheriff still holding Ted Williams?" asked my aunt as she and I began cutting out the fabric around the pinned pattern pieces.

"Yes, but at least I had a chance to speak with Ted earlier today," I said as I laid down my scissors.

Anna and Aunt Fran both paused, each woman questioned me excitedly, their voices blending together. "What did he say? Where was he Saturday night?" The whistle of the teakettle suddenly interrupted.

"Let's take a break; I'll make some tea and we can hear your news," announced Aunt Fran. She set up three mugs on the counter and added a plate of sliced banana nut bread as Anna and I each slid onto a tall bar stool.

"Well, naturally, Ted says he didn't do it and was only trying to help Fred with CPR when I found him. Doug told me the coroner puts the time of death late Sunday morning, probably right before our scouts entered that maze, so Doug being gone Saturday night really doesn't matter," I explained.

"But where was he? I don't like the fact that he left the boys alone," drawled Anna.

"He told me he left for about an hour, and that was to meet someone in the parking lot on Saturday; he wasn't far away."

"Who? Who did he meet? It was a woman, wasn't it?" exclaimed Aunt Fran, slapping her hand on the countertop. "I knew it!"

"Yeah, he said he met a gal that he's been seeing for a while; she drove over to the park. I don't know her name, he wouldn't say, only that she was married."

"Wow, that's interesting. Poor Barb, here she is thinking they'll get back together and old Ted has moved on. Shame," said Aunt Fran.

"I must say, I'm surprised. I thought Ted Williams had more integrity than that. Seeing a married woman... wonder if her husband knows his wife is cheating," Anna said.

"I don't know, and I don't care. That's his private life, as far as I'm concerned. I'm not excusing it, but it doesn't make him a murderer either."

"So, who <u>did</u> do it? Got any ideas?" Anna inquired.

"When we were first talking about the corn maze being at the Granger farm, Anna, you made a comment about the farm being sold. Do you remember where you might have heard that?" I asked.

"Hmm, let me think a minute. Oh yeah, I know. My dental hygienist told me at my cleaning last week. You know, her niece is a teller at the savings and loan office. Nice little gal. I guess Miriam heard it from her niece." Anna said as she added milk to her tea and slowly stirred the cup. "Why?"

"I keep thinking of how many other people around town might have had a motive for killing Fred Granger. I had two other people tell me Fred's property was being sold, but when I asked Ron Wythe about it, he emphatically told me no. Ron underwrites the insurance policy on that farm, and he is also on the planning commission and he swears that no shopping mall was approved, and the Granger farm was not sold," I explained.

"Maybe we should pay a visit to the Knox Savings and Loan and find out more information from that girl," suggested Aunt Fran.

"Do you think she'd talk to us? What's her name?" I asked.

"Um, Charlotte, I think," said Anna.

I took out my notebook from my purse and wrote Charlotte and the bank then added a question mark next to it. Next I added Ted

Williams' name and noted CPR with a question mark. I paused, then jotted down Tilley to my list and drew a large question mark. Anna and Aunt Fran watched with interest as I showed them my notepad.

"What do either of you know about Sam Tilley? I saw and heard him argue with Fred Granger too, a few days before Fred died, and when I tried to ask him about it at the pumpkin farm today, he got nasty with me."

"Don't know much, I agree he's a puzzle. He's been in Meadowood about five years, I think. However, fighting with Fred is certainly suspicious. Wonder what that was all about," pondered Aunt Fran.

"If we want to help Ted Williams, then we have to find the true killer. Ted and Barb both asked for my help, and although I know Doug will be angry with me for meddling in his case, I just can't let an innocent man be accused of murder. What do you think?" I asked.

"I think I should pay a call on Mister Tilley, as one business owner to another, and perhaps talk to him about Chamber business," announced Aunt Fran. "Maybe I can find out what that argument was all about."

"Charlotte will be more likely to talk to me since I know her aunt," said Anna. "Why don't we both go to the bank tomorrow?"

"Okay. I can always pretend to be looking into opening an account for my Avon business. Maybe we can learn why this gal thought the farm was up for sale; where she got her information. Fred Granger's land seems to be in demand, and I can't help but wonder why," I said as I slowly sipped my tea. I underlined Charlotte's name as my thoughts percolated.

"So, we have a plan. Merry, how about you bring Billy over to Anna's house tomorrow evening for a fitting of his costume? Give you a reasonable excuse that Doug won't question, then while the boys are off playing, we can compare notes on what we've learned," said Aunt Fran.

"Okay, that will work. Guess we better get busy sewing these pieces together or we won't have anything to fit," I said.

"You and Anna pin the seams together and hand them to me and I'll stitch these up in no time."

It was close to eleven o'clock when I got home. Doug was awake watching the news on TV and the boys were asleep upstairs. I listened at the foot of the stairs for any sound or cries from Billy before I joined my husband, but all was quiet.

Later that night, close to three o'clock, I awakened to the sound of whimpering. I lay in bed trying to determine whether I had heard an actual sound or if it was merely dream related when I heard the cry again. Now I was certain; a mother knows her child's voice and cry. I jumped out of bed, grabbed a robe and slipped it on as I dashed down the hall to Billy's bedroom. I sat on the side of his bed and gathered him in my arms. I cuddled him with his head resting on my chest and rocked him gently like a baby.

91

"Bad dream? Can you tell me about it?" I asked, patting his back and crooning to him softly.

"It was the bad man. He was chasing me," cried Billy.

"What bad man? You mean like a monster in a dream?"

"No," he whispered and trembled. "The bad man who hurt Mister Granger."

I sat back and gently pulled Billy away from me so I could study his expression in the faint moonlight coming through his bedroom window. The tiny nightlight on the opposite wall illuminated part of his room. His expression visibly and genuinely frightened.

"Can you tell me about the bad man? Mommy and Daddy won't let anyone hurt you, you know that. Tell me about the man."

"I saw him. He hit the old man."

"Then what happened? Did he see you? Do you know the man?" I asked, trying not to let my own fears take hold.

"He grabbed my arm. He told me if I tell anyone what I saw, he'd find me and kill me," Billy cried, great sobs racking his body.

I hugged him tightly and his little hands clutched my robe in an iron grip that could not be broken. I stroked his hair and kissed the top of his head, trying to calm his fears.

A noise in the doorway made me jerk my head around, and I sighed in relief at seeing my husband's familiar silhouette. He stood watching me with Billy before he neared the bed.

"What's wrong? Another bad dream?" Doug asked as he listened to Billy's steady breathing, now broken by a tiny hiccup, as he fell asleep. Billy's thumb was stuck in his mouth. Doug raised questioning eyes to mine.

"Worse. . . Billy witnessed Fred Granger's murder. He's scared to death and now, so am I. What are we going to do?" I whispered.

Chapter 12

Wednesday morning, Frances Andrews performed her opening ritual at the dress shop; hung the open sign on the front door, logged into her computerized cash register, and arranged a trio of sale signs on a rack of knit tops. She looked about and surveyed her small shop with satisfaction, straightened a folded garment here or there, and readied for the day's business to begin.

"Good morning Betty," Fran greeted her young salesgirl.

Betty Jones worked three days a week in the dress shop; a young girl who had just graduated from high school a year ago, she attended the local community college part-time while earning a welcome income at the store. Betty interacted pleasantly with customers and was doing her best to learn the retail business while hoping to pursue a marketing career when her studies ended. Fran smiled at the girl as she watched her arrange a silk scarf about a mannequin's neck and created a more appealing display of the outfit.

"That looks very nice. I have to pop out of the store later to run an errand; can you manage on your own for a while today?" asked Fran.

"Oh sure; we're not normally too busy in the middle of the week. Should be fine," answered Betty.

"Great. Oh, I wanted to show you this new shipment of wool dresses that arrived," Fran said. She motioned Betty to follow her into the rear stock room and opened a large carton.

"Can you work on attaching price tags to these dresses and hang them on a display rack near the front of the store today? I'll be running an ad in this weekend's paper to promote a holiday sale. I think I'll include a photo of these dresses. They'd make an attractive holiday look. Don't you think?"

"Uh huh, sure, no problem. I can work on these while you're in the shop or if I'm not needed up front," Betty replied.

"Thanks. I just want to get 'em on display by the end of the day."

I faced an array of empty cereal bowls, milk glasses, and coffee cups still spread across the breakfast bar. I poured the leftover milk into a bowl for Mittens and started clearing off the mess. The house was finally quiet with Johnny and Doug off to start their day.

I called my mother early in the morning; I knew she'd be awake by at least seven.

"Can you keep Billy for me? I don't want him alone today and I have something that I must do."

"Yes, I guess so. What's wrong? Can you tell me? Did the poor dear have more of those nightmares?"

"Yes, something like that. He just needs to rest. I'll be back by lunch," I said.

After a brief conversation, she agreed to sit with Billy after his harrowing night. I decided he could miss school today and get some

95

much-needed sleep. My mother drove over and picked Billy up, fussing over him and telling him they'd spend the day together.

Doug and I had spent the balance of the night talking and had agreed that the best way to protect Billy was to keep his secret. We could not let anyone else know what he witnessed because it might put him in jeopardy. If the killer thought we could identify him, Billy's life could be in danger. We had to pretend that all was normal. Doug had even more incentive now to find the culprit and swore to me he'd never allow anyone to harm our family.

It was mid-morning as I went about my morning chores while my mind swirled in a tornado of rage. Behaving as if everything was normal would take a level of acting worthy of an academy award. I had just finished loading the dishes into the dishwasher and was drying off my hands on a dish towel when the phone rang and disturbed the silence and my thoughts.

"Mroww," Mittens let me know the loud ring had disrupted his nap as he stretched then sauntered across the kitchen toward his door flap, climbing through to prowl outside on the deck. Immediately, I heard a screech and cry as a pair of cardinals took flight.

I shook my head as I reached for the telephone and stopped the persistent ringing. "Hello. Oh, good morning Anna... No, I haven't forgotten... Okay, if you want to drive, that's fine. I'll be ready outside," I said.

I glanced at the clock and calculated how much more time I had before Anna picked me up at ten o'clock. Hmm, time enough to get the beds made and finish combing my hair and putting on some makeup, so I'd be presentable for our bank outing. It was such a gloomy, rainy day – it matched my mood. I forced myself to think of Ted and the need to find some information to help clear him, and more importantly, my new mission to find who threatened my child.

I ran my fingers through my hair to fluff up my curls and added a touch of mousse to help hold the curls in the wet weather. I slipped on a warm fleece jacket over my green knit top and blue jeans and grabbed an umbrella with my tote bag, then watched for Anna. As soon as I saw her pull in the drive, I dashed out and locked the door behind me.

"Hi," I greeted, as I slid into the passenger seat of her Land Rover.

"Terrible day; isn't it?" asked Anna as she backed out of the driveway and headed toward town.

"Must admit, on days like this I'd rather be snuggled up with a hot cup of tea and a good book. I sure hope it doesn't rain Friday night and spoil trick or treating."

"Mmm, let's keep our fingers crossed," commented Anna.

We drove down Park and pulled into the small lot adjacent to the savings and loan office. As I got out of the car and put up my umbrella, I saw Aunt Fran dash across the street from her shop and head over to us.

"Morning ladies," she called as she approached under the protection of her own bright yellow umbrella. "Ready for a little sleuthing?"

"Yep. You on the way to see Tilley?" I asked.

"Yes. I plan to do my best to get him to open up."

"Well, be careful. See you later tonight," I said.

Anna and I turned toward the entrance of the bank while Aunt Fran proceeded to the butcher shop three doors down. I pushed on the wide glass door and entered the finance office, jiggling my closed umbrella to knock off raindrops onto the tiled entry floor.

Anna tossed back her parka's hood, then brushed a few damp strands of chestnut hair back behind her ears. She nodded toward the teller standing at the far left of the counter, indicating she was Charlotte. Anna pasted a smile on her face as she walked toward the teller's window and I followed close behind.

"Hello Charlotte!" Anna greeted warmly. "How are you today?"

"I'm fine, thank you," Charlotte replied pleasantly but hesitantly. I could see by her expression she was trying to place where she knew us from since Anna had used her name.

"I was just speaking with your aunt Miriam the other day. She's such a sweet person. I told her my friend here needed some place that she could trust with her business and naturally Miriam suggested we come speak with you," Anna explained and smiled again with a quick wink to me.

"Oh, I see," Charlotte replied with a more friendly smile, evidently relieved that she had not forgotten someone important. "What can I help you with?"

I stepped forward and, following Anna's lead, tried to appear nervous and lost. "I have a small business, nothing much really, but I want to open a separate checking account for my business, so I don't get money mixed up with my personal account. I suppose keeping cash and receipts in a shoe box just won't do any more. Is there someone I can talk to?"

"I'm sure we can assist you."

"My husband takes care of our household budget, so I'm just not too sure what needs to be done." I cast my eyes downward and fumbled with my purse, then stealthily slipped my cell phone into my pocket. I watched as she buzzed the manager's desk and quietly spoke into the intercom.

"Mr. Logan, our manager, opens new accounts. Perhaps he can explain our services to you. He'll be able to see you in just a minute."

"Well, that's just perfect, ain't it Merry?" Anna beamed. "I'll just spend a moment visiting with Charlotte while you're busy. I've got some business to transact, anyway."

"Thank you," I said as I moved toward the enclosed area tucked away in the rear corner of the building. A short, two-foot high knee wall held glass above it up to the ceiling and allowed a view of the manager's office containing a desk and file cabinets along one wall. An artificial potted fiddle-leaf fig tree stood in one corner. Dust covered

99

the broad, flat plastic leaves. An array of certificates and awards were displayed on the one solid wall, their cheap black frames hung crookedly.

An older, gray-haired man stood and walked toward the doorway, ready to welcome me.

"Hello. Harry Logan, branch manager, how can I help you today?" He extended his hand in a friendly but limp handshake and waved me forward. "Please have a chair, Missus ...?"

"Gardner. Mrs. Meredith Gardner," I introduced myself as I moved past the short stout man, then perched primly on the edge of the chair closest to the front of his desk. I juggled my wet umbrella and bag, placing both of them on the floor by my feet. I gave him a timid smile and hoped I would appear like a shy, helpless housewife. I waited for him to speak as my eyes darted to the mounds of papers strewn on his desk.

The banker sat down on his swivel chair; his elbows rested on the desktop as he laced his fingers together, creating a steeple affect. He picked up a pen and nervously fiddled with it, dropped it twice, then laid it aside before flattening his palms on the desk blotter.

"Hmm, Gardner... any relationship to Deputy Douglas Gardner?" Logan asked.

"Well, yes. He's my husband. Is that a problem?"

"Oh no, just thought the name sounded familiar, that's all," he fretted. "Um, so, I understand you want to open a new checking account and you've chosen us. Tell me about your business."

I decided it would be smarter to stick with the truth as much as possible when I answered his questions, otherwise I could get tripped up in my own lies. Let him believe I was just another silly little woman with her unimportant hobby business. It would give him a feeling of superiority, perhaps cause him to let his guard down.

"Well, I sell Avon cosmetics. It's just a small business, you understand, not really much more than a hobby, but it gives me extra spending money. I was thinking I'd be more professional if I had a real business account for it," I said quietly, my voice trailed off as I folded my hands in my lap and then moved them to rest on the corner of his desk as I leaned forward and tried to read upside down some of the closer documents.

"I see. Of course, we can help you. I have some brochures here that will describe our various plans. Did you want to open the account today? How many names will be on the account?" asked the manager.

"Um, I'm not sure. Can I read what the minimum deposit is and what your fees are?" I replied, giving him a bashful look and casting my eyes downward.

"Of course, yes of course, you'll want to examine the details. Now let me see, I have a pamphlet that describes our basic checking account that should meet your needs. Hmm, it should be right here... I don't see it. Just give me a minute, I'll get one from the tellers. Be right back," Logan said as he jumped up and left the office.

I quickly leaned forward and spun a stack of paperwork around so I could read it easier. I leafed through two pages quickly, then slowed as my eyes scanned names on a report of ACH direct deposits received from the Federal Reserve into the savings and loan branch. Fred Granger's name was on the list. I grabbed my cell phone from my pocket and snapped a picture of the page. Another page detailed escrow accounts, so I snapped a photo of that one too before I slid the paperwork back into position and resumed my seat. I glanced over my shoulder and spied Harry Logan walking back to his office. I prayed he didn't notice me rummaging through his desk.

"Here we are, Mrs. Gardner," the manager said as he handed me a colorful brochure.

"Thank you so much for your time, Mister Logan. I'd like to read this through and come back in, if that's okay with you?"

"Perfectly fine, my dear. I'll be here to help you when you're ready. I'm sure you'll be happy doing business with Knox Savings and Loan. You can be assured your money is safe with us," he grinned and gave me that limp handshake again.

I scooped up my bag and umbrella, then hurried over to Anna where she waited in the lobby. I nudged her and we both left the office as quickly as we could.

"Whew!" I breathed a sigh of relief. "I thought he was going to catch me for sure. I saw some interesting papers on his desk, maybe nothing, but how could anyone have their home go up for sheriff sale for unpaid taxes when their mortgage is paid by direct deposit?"

"That's what Charlotte said when I was able to casually ask her about the Granger farm being for sale. She pulled up the Granger account on her computer screen. Naturally, I couldn't see what she did, but then she frowned and said that was funny because she saw all these payments posted. So how come the taxes weren't paid? Do you think she'll blab to her boss about our questions?" Anna worried.

"I hope not. I don't want Logan to get suspicious while we're investigating. Let's run by the sheriff's office. Do you have time?" I asked.

"Okay. I've got plenty of time before I have to be home," replied Anna. "What are we looking for?"

"I want to see a list of the properties listed for sale and auction by the sheriff for nonpayment of taxes. Something doesn't jive."

Anna drove down the street and turned onto Broad, parking in the visitor's lot next to the sheriff's office. The rain had stopped, but the sky still appeared cloudy and the temperature had dropped significantly. I pulled my collar up closer against my neck as I dashed into the office while Anna waited in the car.

I was in luck as I pulled open the heavy glass door and spotted Tony Dalton on duty at the front desk. I hated taking advantage of the young man and the crush he had on me, but how else could I get information out of the police office? I squashed my guilt feelings as his face lit up when he saw me approach. He sprung to his feet; his chair shot backwards and careened into the wall. The loud crash startled him, causing him to knock over his half-empty coffee cup. He frantically grabbed to move papers out of harm's way as the liquid spread across the desk blotter.

"Oh dear! Let me help," I cried as I picked up documents and dabbed at the wet mess on his desk with a wad of tissues. Now I felt guilty all over again. I didn't know I had that kind of effect on him.

"Thanks Mrs... ah, Merry. Sorry. I seem to be clumsy today," said Tony, his face blushing in embarrassment.

"No problem, Tony. We all have our moments."

"Did you need to see your husband?" he asked as he tossed the soggy tissues into a trash can.

"Actually Tony, it was you I came to see today," I informed him with a big smile and prayed it didn't start another catastrophe.

"Me?" he squeaked, flustered. "Ah, me? What can I help you with?"

"I'd like to see a copy of the current properties up for sheriff sale this month. Can you get me a copy, please?"

"Sure! I can do that," he beamed at me, his confidence obviously restored.

"I was certain you could. Those listings are your responsibility, aren't they?"

"Yes ma'am. I update the sale listings and schedule the auction dates."

"Thank you. I just want to browse through the real estate listings; see what's available for a friend," I told him as I reached for the two-page photocopy. "My goodness, there seems to be quite a few properties."

"Yeah, the courthouse sent over more names and addresses than usual this month. I wonder why?" Tony mumbled as he scratched his head. "Anything else I can do for you, Merry?"

"No thank you, Tony. You've been a dear. This is all I need. You have a good day now. Thanks again," I said with a smile as I turned to go.

I climbed back into Anna's Land Rover and we head back into town. Anna glanced down at the pages I was tucking into my tote.

"Get what you need?" she asked.

"I've got the latest inventory of properties going up for sale. I wanted to see if the sheriff has the Granger farm on it," I told Anna.

"And does it?"

"Afraid so."

"Well, where to? Home or a quick coffee and donut at Martha's?" suggested Anna.

"A hot cup of anything right now sounds good. I'm chilled to the bone in this damp air. Let's go to Martha's and see what she's baked today."

"Reckon that's a plan," drawled Anna as she headed toward our favorite bakery and coffee shop.

"Hello, I'm Frances Andrews. I own a little dress shop, Frannie's Frocks, just down the street. In all the time you've been here, I don't think we've had a chance to formally meet."

105

Sam Tilley dried his hands on a towel and studied the striking woman standing in front of him. He'd noticed her around town; hard to miss the shapely blonde. He eyed her suspiciously, wondering why she was here.

"What can I do for you, lady?"

"Please, call me Fran. As a fellow merchant, I just wanted to stop by. I don't believe I've ever seen you at our Chamber of Commerce meetings. Have I?"

"I don't attend those things," answered Sam gruffly.

"Well... I'm chairperson of a local food drive for the homeless and poor. I was hoping you might volunteer some time to help with the food drive?" Fran asked as she watched his face and tried to read his expression.

"Too busy to leave the shop. I'll donate something. What do you need?"

"Oh, that's too bad, I was looking forward to working with you," Fran cajoled. "Perhaps you could donate some canned goods or a monetary contribution?"

"Yeah, I'll see what I can do," Tilley scowled.

"Thank you. My, you do have some nice cuts of meat in that case, Sam. May I call you Sam?" Fran asked in a honey-toned voice.

Caught off guard by her flirtatious manner, Sam wasn't certain how to react. He shuffled his feet and looked at her again. It had been a long time since he'd been with a woman; he was no monk and not immune to the musky scent of her perfume or the way she tossed her blond silky hair off her shoulder.

Fran stood quietly, waiting for an answer. She noticed a subtle shift in his manner, a softening toward her. She pressed her advantage.

"Sam, do you sell only local meat from our neighboring farms?"

"What? Yeah, mostly, when we can agree on a fair price. You looking for something special?" he asked.

"Maybe. I like to know where my food comes from, that's all, and I prefer to support my local businesses. For instance, Ross Farm grows some of the best pumpkins and squash. Did you know they make their own apple butter too? They have a wonderful apple orchard."

"Yeah, I've been there."

"Oh, that's good. I like their produce. How about your chicken? Is that from a local farm?" Fran asked.

"I get my chicken from an Amish farm, Yoders, up in Butler County."

"You have some lovely pork chops and roasts. Do you deal with the Granger farm for your pork? I think he's the largest pig farm in this area," Fran said and watched his reaction.

"Granger, yeah, most of the pork is his. Damn old man always wants to fight me on the price," Sam said, his voice louder.

Fran took a risk and pressed him for an answer. "Was that what you and Fred were arguing about last week?"

"He accused me of cheating him on the price of two stupid pigs. Me! Like I'd steal from him!" Tilley raged.

107

Fran studied the tall man standing before her. His muscular torso and upper arms strained against the stained white smock he wore. His dark wavy hair grew long in the back, brushing against his collar while trim sideburns hugged his flushed cheek. He looked like an experienced man that could take a woman's breath away if she wasn't put off by his sudden sparks of temper.

"You don't look like a man who would do that. What happened?" Fran questioned, her voice oozed concern.

"Nothing. He threatened to go to the sheriff. I knew he was all hot air. I can prove what I paid, and he damn well knew it."

"You strike me as an honorable man, Sam Tilley," Fran spoke quietly. She had decided to view Sam as an attractive man and not a potential suspect. Her niece, Merry, was all wrong in her opinion of this good-looking and available male.

His head jerked up at her tone and he studied her closely. What's her game? He wanted to call her bluff and see what happens.

"Maybe we can go out to dinner some night?" he invited.

"Maybe we can," Fran breathed. Smiling, she slid her business card across the counter toward him, then turned to leave as she smiled seductively. "Call me."

Chapter 13

"Aunt Fran! I can't believe you did that! How could you agree to go on a date with that strange man?" I shrieked in disbelief.

We had gathered around the kitchen table to share our investigative findings Wednesday evening. Billy and I had walked over to Anna's house after dinner so his spaceman costume could have a final fitting. As soon as I marked the hem line on his pants, Billy scooted upstairs to play video games with Stevie. It relieved me to see him behave normally again. We girls pulled out our notes to confer.

"Relax, Merry. I only told him *maybe;* really, he seemed like a decent guy. I honestly think his argument with Fred Granger was over prices. I can't see him escalating that to violence," Aunt Fran speculated.

"Are you sure? You really don't think he was involved in Fred's murder? No one in town knows anything about Sam Tilley. Where did he come from before he moved to Meadowood? Why doesn't he have any friends or family visit?" I inquired.

"Maybe I can find out answers to all those questions if I do go out to dinner with him," teased Aunt Fran. She grinned at me, then stuck out her tongue and made a face.

"You're incorrigible, you know that? As my elder, you're supposed to set a better example for me," I joked and made a face right back at her.

Anna laughed at the two of us. "Okay, so what else did we learn today? Merry, show us that report you found on Logan's desk."

"It's a little blurry around the edges; I printed out the photo I took with my phone. This report shows some direct deposit funds that the savings and loan received and cross references to loan numbers. So, I think it means a customer's loan would have been paid automatically. The bank would have to break down the payment and apply it toward principle, interest and escrow accounts. See what I mean?" I asked as we all examined the report figures.

"Fred Granger's name is on this list," Anna pointed out.

"Yes, it is. Now we don't know for sure if the loan number listed on this report means his mortgage, it could have been a car loan for all I know," I said, circling Fred's name with a yellow highlighter.

Aunt Fran snorted, "A new car loan? Not hardly! Did you ever see the junker Fred drove? That old pickup must have at least two hundred thousand miles on it."

Anna spoke up, "I asked the teller, Charlotte, about the Granger farm being for sale and she peeked at his bank account and told me she didn't understand why it would be reported for back taxes when his account postings show paid up to date."

"Wow, that's interesting," commented Aunt Fran as she studied the report again. "What's that other paper?" she asked as she picked up the second image I had printed.

"Oh, that one is an escrow account report that I found on Logan's desk. See the categories for homeowner's insurance, mortgage insurance premiums and real estate taxes? There are numerous debit accounts identified there," I explained.

"Listen to you; those accounting courses you took in college are paying off," laughed Aunt Fran.

"Aww, now you're embarrassing me. Hey, I stopped at the sheriff's office and got a copy of the properties going up for sale this month. I'm curious if the Granger Farm is the only one that has this discrepancy of paid balances at the bank but unpaid accounts with the county. I think I'll try and cross reference how many names on this bank list are on the sheriff's. What if Fred Granger suddenly learned his farm was being announced for sale because the bank had not paid his taxes? Doug told me Fred argued with Harry Logan the week before his death. Do you think Logan could have killed Fred?"

"More likely Fred Granger would want to throttle Harry Logan if he found out something like that," commented Aunt Fran. "I know that's how I'd feel if that happened to me."

"Well, it's something to think about. Logan may have had a very good motive for wanting Fred dead. He was awfully antsy when I was in his office and extremely nervous when he learned my husband was a deputy."

I tried to picture Harry Logan hitting Fred Granger with a shovel; would he be the type of man to threaten a child too? I wasn't sure I could see him in that role, but you never could tell.

"I still have to research the clerk of court records open to the public on some of these properties. I should be able to find out what taxes were paid and when, or what kind of liens are filed on a given address. I can search online for most of this stuff because I don't have time to go to the courthouse in Mount Vernon," I continued, as I gathered my documents. "Here's a thought, what if it is someone in the clerk of court's office that's stealing the money?"

"Oh my, I never considered that possibility. Hey, I saw Fred's obituary in the paper today; the family is hosting calling hours tomorrow evening with a private burial on Friday. Are you going?" Anna asked Aunt Fran and me.

"I may have to close the shop early, but I'll be there," Aunt Fran said. "Fred Granger and his family have lived in this area for a good many years. He'd always been a kind man; he only got grumpy after Louise died."

"Doug will probably attend; the sheriff's office will want to have a presence there; try to spot someone looking suspicious or guilty, I guess. But I think I should go with the boys, they're old enough now to understand and they need to show their respect. Fred Granger supported our scout troop over the years, plus he created that corn maze for all the kids to enjoy. It's the least I can do. Besides, Doug won't be the only one watching for someone acting guilty."

"The paper said calling hours were from seven o'clock until nine at Wagner's Funeral Home," stated Anna.

"I guess Fred's son and daughter must be back in town. I haven't seen Pam in years, but Allen has been in and out," Aunt Fran mused.

"You'll need to point them out to me; I doubt I'd recognize either of them," I said. "Thanks for going with me today, Anna. I better round up Billy and get home."

"See you both tomorrow," Aunt Fran stated.

"Tomorrow will be a busy day," I said as Billy and I took our leave.

I arranged four pots of bronze and yellow chrysanthemums with the pumpkins that Billy and Johnny had created. One pumpkin with a pair of mums sat on each side of our hunter green front door to give our house a nice Halloween decoration. I stood back and admired the holiday grouping. *"Yes, very nice,"* I thought, pleased.

Our rainy weather had departed early Thursday morning, leaving behind frosty temperatures in its wake. I rubbed my hands together to warm them as I walked back into our kitchen, still toasty from the raisin bran muffins I had baked earlier. Even Mittens must be feeling the cold; he jumped through his pet door onto the deck outside but dashed back into the house within a few minutes.

"Too cold, huh?" I asked, as I watched my furry baby knead his cat bed and turn around a few times until he had the perfect soft spot in which to nap.

113

"Rowww," Mittens answered me as he tucked his head under a paw.

I tossed another log onto the crackling fire; the lit fireplace helped to take the chill out of the room as I settled down in front of my laptop screen. I opened up Google and decided to do a search on one Samuel Tilley to learn more about him. I typed in his name as both Sam and Samuel, but no matches. The only hit was on the name of the butcher shop. I tried again by searching public records, birth records, even Ancestry came up empty. It was as if he didn't exist. How odd. What can that mean? I tried entering his name in as many search engines as I could think of, but still no results. Finally, I gave up and shifted my efforts to the bank records in question.

With pen in hand and notebook open, I logged onto the county website and started my search for real estate tax billings. I stared at my laptop screen as I scrolled through the quarterly tax bills for the bank customer names printed on the report. I held the sheriff sale list in one hand and circled names common on both reports. How could this be correct? The bank records show all these accounts as being current, yet the county included them on their delinquent list. Something is definitely not right here. Hmm, I wonder...

I grabbed the telephone book and ran my finger down the column of names then across and jotted down the phone number for the first person on my report. Dialing the number, I held my breath as I waited for the person to pick up and wondered what I'd say when they did.

"Hello, Mister Carson? Hi, my name is Meredith Gardner. Do you have a moment?"

"Hello Missus Gardner. What can I do for you?" Carson asked.

"Um, I was just calling, um, because I saw your home included in this month's sheriff auctions and I wanted to know more about the property," my voice faltered as I worried what his reaction would be.

"I don't know what you're talking about. I can assure you my house is not for sale by me and certainly, not the sheriff. I'm afraid you've got some wrong information," Carson grumbled.

"Well, I'm happy to hear that Mr. Carson, but you might want to speak with the sheriff's office and make sure they do correct their records," I suggested.

"How did you say you found this information? I appreciate your phone call; I wouldn't have known anything until it was too late."

"My husband is a deputy. I picked up a copy of the current sales report from the station when I was there a few days ago. Perhaps the county records are in error and they gave Sheriff Simmons false data. I hope I didn't upset you," I fretted.

"No, no, I'm more angry than I'm upset, but I plan on getting to the bottom of this, I can tell you!"

"I think that would be a good idea, Mr. Carson. Thank you for your time."

"Thank you, Missus Gardner. I'm going to phone the sheriff right now."

115

I hung up and studied both reports again, then drew a big question mark next to the Carson name. I searched for the next name and address on the auction report and found the same name among the savings and loan customers again. My fingers rifled through pages of the phone book as I sought a phone number.

This time I dialed the number with more confidence. I was determined to discover how many more homeowners were unaware that they were in danger of losing their homes.

"Hello, Missus Hollinger, my name is Meredith Gardner."

"Hi Meredith, aren't you the Avon sales lady in town?" the woman asked.

"Yes ma'am, I am. However, I'm not calling about Avon today. I wanted to ask you if you knew your home was listed for sale by the sheriff for delinquent taxes."

"What?!" she screamed into my ear. "That can't be right."

"Well, I didn't think so Missus Hollinger, but I saw your name on a new sales report for homes going on auction and I thought I would warn you. I've found a few mistakes on the county tax records and have been looking into the matter," I explained.

"Why?" Hollinger asked suspiciously. "Why should you be concerned?"

"Well, um, I guess that's a good question. I'm sort of investigating a problem with payment records between the savings and loan and county tax records. If you are sure that your balance is paid in full, I'd recommend that you contact Sheriff Simmons and get your records updated."

"I most certainly will, and Harry Logan will hear from me too. My mortgage payment is paid by an automatic withdrawal from my checking account every month; it's never late," insisted Missus Hollinger.

"I'm sure you're right, Mrs. Hollinger. Thank you for your time today," I said and hung up.

Scanning the county tax listings, I compared the bank report and the sales list and found two more names. When I telephoned them, I received similar responses. All the Knox S & L customers had mortgages paid by direct deposit, but mysteriously, none of their real estate taxes had been forwarded to the county, causing all of their properties to be reported as delinquent. The county clerk of court had identified all of these homes as being behind in their property taxes for over a year. So where was all the money? The bank records indicated everyone's account as current.

I was pondering the problem when Doug rushed into the house at noon. He doesn't normally come home for lunch. By the harried expression on his face, I knew all was not well.

"What are you doing?" he barked.

"Is something wrong?" I asked innocently.

"In the past hour, Simmons' phone has been ringing off the wall with angry residents all wanting to know how their home got on our auction list. They all mentioned they were informed of the problem by one Meredith Gardner! Now I ask you again, what the hell are you doing?" Doug demanded.

"No need to curse at me, dear. Maybe you better sit down so I can share some things with you." I got up and poured him a mug of coffee as he took off his hat and tossed it onto an empty chair. I spread out three documents before him on the table with my notes written along the margins in red ink.

Doug read the reports, laid one next to another, then raised his eyebrows as he studied the documents closer.

"Where did you get these? What made you look into this? Do you have any idea the bedlam you've created?" he asked in a calmer voice.

"Well... it all started with the rumor that Fred Granger's farm was being sold. Remember Ron telling me that he would have known if the Granger farm was being sold for development? He said right here the night of our dinner party that Fred wasn't selling out. But then Anna told me a teller at the bank said that it was. It got me curious. So, I, ah, kind of visited the bank one day and talked with the manager, Harry Logan. I accidentally saw this report on his desk with Fred Granger's name on it and, well, I took a picture of it."

"You mean you stole private, confidential banking information?" accused Doug.

"Gosh, honey, when you put it like that... but see, here's his name on your sheriff sale and how can that be if the bank record shows his account all paid up? One of these has to be wrong. I thought if I checked with the court records that the real truth would be found. The only problem is, the court records show him delinquent too.”

“Let me see that report again.”

“If you look at the properties listed with the county and sheriff for back taxes, all of those properties are mortgaged with Knox Savings and Loan. Don’t you think that’s odd?”

“Yes, it’s odd, but it is also a case for a bank examiner, not you. Whatever made you contact all these people?” Doug questioned me again as he ran his hand through his hair. He raised his eyes to me and shook his head.

“I just wondered if what I was seeing was true, that’s all. Do you know that none of the people I called had the faintest idea their homes were in jeopardy? How could that happen? Don’t you think your office should look into the matter?” I asked. I stood with my hands on my hips and stared right back at him.

He laughed at my efforts to appear indignant. “Come here. You know I can’t stay mad at you for long. The boss is furious, and he’ll want a full explanation, but I suppose these folks should thank you for being incorrigibly nosy.” He wrapped me in a bear hug and nuzzled my neck.

I sighed as I enjoyed his show of affection, then suddenly pushed him away as I recalled the point I wanted to make.

“Doug, don’t you think it’s suspicious that Fred Granger had an argument with Harry Logan and then a few days later is found dead? What if Logan is embezzling and Fred caught him? What if Logan

119

killed him to keep him quiet? Do you think Logan is the bad man that Billy saw?"

"Would definitely give Logan a motive for murder, all right. But didn't you promise me you would not get involved investigating? And here you are, up to your eyeballs stealing bank documents and stirring up trouble," Doug said.

"How can I not when someone is frightening my child? I can't just stand by and do nothing. So, what are you going to do about Harry Logan?" I persisted.

"I'll look into it. I promise. I keep my word, unlike some people," he said with a frown and a stern look cast in my direction.

"Really?"

"Yeah, really. Now stay out of police business, will you?"

"Are you going to release Ted Williams? Doesn't he deserve the benefit of the doubt with all this other evidence?" I asked.

"As a matter of fact, Ted was released on bail this morning."

"Oh. Well, that's good." My indignation totally deflated. "You of all people must realize that Ted didn't do it; not if Billy saw the *bad man* and it wasn't his scout leader."

"I agree, but we've got to keep that fact to ourselves for a while longer. Now, I've got to get back to the office. I'm taking these documents; Simmons will be interested to see what all the fuss has been about. I'll see you later."

"Are you on duty at the funeral home tonight? I was planning on stopping by with the boys to pay our respects."

"You aren't up to anything are you? Just pay respects and leave, right?" he asked with a hint of suspicion.

"We'll be in and out. I wish you would trust me more, makes me feel like a criminal," I scoffed.

"Humph, see you later. Stay out of trouble."

"Not likely; not while there's a murderer out there who's stalking my son!" I whispered to myself.

Chapter 14

Orange and black crepe paper dangled from the cafeteria door frame as I reached for a new roll of scotch tape to secure it. Carol, Anna, and I had volunteered to decorate the school cafeteria for tomorrow night's Halloween celebration. Joseph Cooper had finished cleaning up from the earlier lunch period, so the room was now ours to decorate in spooky goblins and Halloween colors. I twisted strands of crepe paper, twirling the ends and adding the string to the edge of two treat tables. Paper jack-o'-lanterns perched upon the cafeteria serving counters. Fuzzy pipe-cleaner black spiders hung by threads from ceiling tiles and swayed in the warm air blowing out of heat registers. Construction paper orange pumpkin faces and black cats peeked out of every windowpane.

Meadowood Elementary contained a cornerstone block that read *Built in 1902*. The older, square brick building rose three floors tall above a full basement that included a labyrinth of pipes and huge octopus-like heater ducts. It had been my own elementary school from kindergarten to sixth grade. As a kid, I climbed up and down those tall staircases going to class or ran around outside on the playground, delighted in climbing the monkey bars or riding the swings. I remember once, as a young child probably seven or eight years old, I got lost in the basement. I wandered from electrical room to steam room to maintenance and thought I would never find my way out again. Luckily for me, Mister Holden, the janitor at the time, saved me from a fate worse than death. Unfortunately, he couldn't save me from the spanking I received when I got home from parents who had been scared out of their wits. I often recall that childhood experience when I have to work in the school building that has now become so familiar to me. Carol's voice questioning a second time broke my reverie and brought me back to the present.

"Think the kids will like it?" Carol asked. She stuffed balled up newspapers into torn blue jean legs as she worked to give her scarecrow a full body.

"Here you go, tie this rope belt around the waist and let's tuck in the ends of his flannel shirt. Handsome fella, don't you think?" laughed Anna. Both worked to plump up the scarecrow figure with more crumpled paper and finished with bunches of straw sticking out of his wrists and neck.

"Great job, ladies," complimented Colleen as she surveyed the party room.

"Thanks," I replied. "We just need to finish our friend there, attach a head, and prop him up somewhere. We'll be done soon."

"Someone keep an eye on the clock; I've got to have time to get changed before Fred's viewing tonight," commented Anna.

"Me too. I'll probably have a fight with the boys about wearing their Sunday school clothes on a weeknight. However, you know who will win or they won't go trick or treating," I exclaimed.

"Ooh, you're mean," laughed Carol.

123

"Sometimes a mom's gotta do what a mom has to do," I quoted and giggled. "Of course, I know they won't believe me, and I probably wouldn't call their bluff, but I do have to save face."

"Anything new on you know what?" asked Anna in her loud whisper, causing Carol to glance our way from across the room.

"Nothing much, except Sheriff Simmons has been fending off telephone calls and complaints from angry homeowners. It seems someone informed them about their homes being in jeopardy of confiscation for sale," I chuckled and rolled my eyes.

"Oh, my goodness, you didn't?" exclaimed Anna.

"I thought Doug would explode when he found out."

"So now what happens?"

"Doug commandeered all my paperwork and research, then took it back to the station with him to show Simmons. He says they will confront Harry Logan and question the discrepancies."

"Wow, I don't know whether we helped solve Fred's murder, but I feel like we did a good deed anyway," pondered Anna. "Don't you?"

"I guess so. At least we may have saved some folk's homes. I'm still not sure about Logan though; he could have killed Fred."

"He seems too mealy mouth to me; I can't picture him having the courage to attack a big man like Fred Granger."

"Somebody sure did. Someone that Fred must have trusted and allowed to get close to him. Now that I think of it, I didn't see any defensive wounds on his arms or hands," I said.

"Hmm, you've got a point. Hey, I've got to go. I'll catch up with you later at Wagner's."

"All right, Anna. I think we're done here. I'll just help Carol pick up and I'll be leaving too."

The boys surprised me by not putting up too much of a fuss as they dressed in their Sunday best suits. I gave them one last inspection before we left the house. I bent down and adjusted Johnny's click on tie so it would hang straight, then tucked in Billy's shirttail into his waistband. They both had added wool sweater vests under their suit jackets for warmth.

"You both look very nice. I'm so proud of you," I said as I kissed each on the forehead. "I promise you we won't have to stay long but it is proper to pay our respects to Mister Granger's family."

"Okay, Mom," they both chorused.

"Thank you, all you have to do is say hello or if you want, just stand quietly while I extend our condolences to the family."

I adjusted the silk scarf tied about the neckline of my charcoal gray wool dress. A quick glance in the hall mirror allowed me to check on my hair, finger combing a stray curl that defied my hairstyle. I swear, my hair has a mind of its own at times. Sighing, I tucked a few tendrils behind my ears to expose silver filigree earrings. I nodded at my reflection, then picked up a slim black clutch that matched my black pumps. I wanted a conservative yet fashionable outfit for the somber

125

occasion. I grabbed car keys then slipped wallet and cell phone into the purse; it didn't feel natural to be traveling light tonight without my usual tote bag stuffed to the gills. Quickly donning my winter coat, I shut off lights as we left the house and clicked the lock behind me.

Billy and Johnny were both unusually subdued as we drove the short distance to Wagner's Funeral Home. Normally I had to remind them to stop squabbling or fidgeting. I glanced in the rearview mirror and studied the worried expressions and frowns upon their youthful faces.

"Hey guys, it'll be okay."

"I know, Mom," Johnny uttered.

I noticed Johnny reach over to squeeze his brother's hand in comfort. I wondered if Billy had confided in his older brother about the bad man. It would be typical of Johnny to assume the role of protector, even at his youthful age. Those little shoulders carried more responsibility than they should. The thought brought a tear to my eye, and I hastily wiped it away.

Wagner's Funeral Home was located in a prominent Victorian structure painted an ominous gray with black trimmed windows, and complete with turrets and gables on its three-story high roof; it had once been home to a wealthy investor in the late 1800s. Like many expansive older homes, they were impossible to heat or cool and wound up being sold for some type of commercial use. The gothic designed house could be spooky enough in daylight, but at night, it seemed like a place straight out of a Stephen King novel. The only thing missing was a gargoyle atop one of the gables.

As I neared Wagner's, the volume of cars lining both sides of the street surprised me. I pulled into the customer parking lot and drove slowly up and down its three rows but didn't see any open spots. Every space was full. Back onto the street again, I cruised slowly, looking for an opening along the curb. Finally, I spied a car pulling into the street and hurried to grab his vacated parking space. We would have to walk the two blocks back to the funeral home, but it appeared to be the closest I could get. Practicing my rusty parallel parking skills, I managed to maneuver my minivan into the slot.

"Okay boys; looks like we have to hoof it. It's cold out there, so no dawdling."

I grabbed my purse, locked the car, and took Billy's hand in mine as we hustled down the street. Johnny kept pace right next to me and we only paused once in our stride to check traffic before crossing the street in front of Wagner's.

A rush of warm air enveloped us as we entered the wide doors of the funeral parlor. The welcome heat quickly became stuffy and cloying in the close confines. Throngs of people stood speaking softly or shuffling around to greet others they hadn't seen in ages or not since the last community event. We inched our way forward in a slow-moving line toward the guest book resting upon a dark walnut lectern. Over-powering waves of heavy colognes from over a hundred people mixed with sweet floral scents radiating from the adjoining room where multiple baskets displayed heady arrangements of roses, carnations, goldenrod, lilies and mums tucked into sprays of autumn leaves. The combined fragrances clung to the heated atmosphere.

I signed the book, expressing sympathy from the Gardner family, then ushered the boys into the main visitation room. Heavy navy-blue brocaded draperies were drawn closed across a triple wide window. Several rows of folding chairs had been set up on the plush slate-colored carpeting in the middle of the spacious room, with comfortable sofas and brocade side chairs arranged along the outer walls. I strained to see more, raising up on my tippy toes to see above the heads of the crowd. I spotted Fred's coffin resting on its stand. Thank God it was a closed coffin. Two framed photographs rested atop the flag-draped casket. I could just make out one as a younger picture of Fred in Army uniform and the other seemed more recent and reminded me of a photo taken of Fred at one of his harvest parties.

Perusing the room, I glimpsed two people seated near the head of the casket and surrounded by towns people; I assumed it must be Fred's son and daughter. I wish I could have gotten a better look at them, but we were standing so far back near the entrance that I could not see very well. A sizeable crowd of people blocked my view as we tried to crawl forward. I saw Colleen mixing with the crowd and noted that Ron Wythe stood beside her. I couldn't help but smile over that. I searched for more friends in the gathering.

A snatch of conversation caught my attention and caused me to crane my neck and scan the throng again.

"Well, he has his nerve, showing up here. I heard Ted Williams was out on bail," a man's voice growled.

"Imagine that," the woman with him sneered.

I finally caught sight of Ted; Barb faithfully stood by his side, clutching his hand and lending support to her ex-husband. Both appeared uncomfortable but determined. Their son Joey wore a stoic expression as he waited with them. I waved and Ted must have seen me because he lifted his hand slightly in acknowledgement.

Billy and Johnny stood before me, and I placed my hand on Billy's shoulder to guide him along as the reception line inched forward. I read the names on various gift cards attached to the flowery devotions, some I recognized and some I did not. I spotted Anna and Chuck standing across the room. She waved a hello, but it was impossible to reach them in this mass. I glanced around, my eyes searching for other familiar faces. I wondered if Aunt Fran had arrived yet.

As we moved forward, I was shocked to see Sam Tilley in the room. I tried to get Anna's attention to point him out, but she had turned to speak with Martha Parker. It appeared the entire town had turned out to honor Fred Granger, then it occurred to me that the Granger family was likely a founder of Meadowood. Their family has claimed this area as home for at least four generations.

The muted voices buzzing in the room suddenly hushed as an Army honor guard marched into the room; the rat-tat-tat of a small drum sounded as people moved and cleared a path for them. Heels clicked smartly as they came to an abrupt stop at the foot of the coffin

129

bier. They turned to face their fallen comrade, then saluted. One soldier raised his trumpet and blew *Taps;* the hauntingly melancholy sound echoed across the silence in the room.

Billy and Johnny watched spellbound as the military ceremony concluded. Another salute to the family members, then the honor guard pivoted and exited the room in a quick march.

"Was Mister Granger in the Army, Mom?" asked Johnny in awe.

"Yes, I believe he was. I didn't know it myself until I read his obituary in the newspaper today. He fought in the Vietnam War a long time ago," I explained.

"What's an obit...airy? That word you said," Billy whispered.

"That's what the newspaper calls a story they write about someone's life when that person dies," I said.

Around us the crowd had started murmuring again and our procession line moved. I shifted my attention from the boys and again searched the crowd for my husband or aunt. I nodded and smiled briefly in acknowledgement to several acquaintances when I noticed Harry Logan also in attendance. What was he doing here? I suppose it might be natural that he'd come; Fred was a customer, after all. But still...

As we came nearer to the front of the room, Billy suddenly tugged frantically on my hand. His eyes were wide as saucers and he gulped soundlessly as he tried to get the words out.

"What's wrong? Are you afraid of the coffin?" I asked as I held him close to my side, trying not to draw attention to us. I decided I had to get Billy away from the press of people and whatever had frightened him. We turned and pushed our way through the throng; my goal to leave that stifling room and head for the exit.

Once we were outside the frigid air washed over us and I took a deep cleansing breath. I crouched down and held Billy against me. I felt his little heart pounding inside his chest; the pallor on his face frightened me. I glanced at Johnny and could see his brother's reaction had scared him too.

"What is it, Billy? Can you tell Mommy?"

He could only shake his head as tears flowed, and sobs racked his body.

"You'll be all right. Let's go home."

We almost ran the two blocks to the car. Billy's fears were contagious; I'd never seen him like that... except the day in the corn maze. My hand shook as I tried to jam the key into the lock. I felt a palpable need to be home. The boys climbed into the rear van seat and cowered together as I started the engine and raced down the street toward home.

"Bad man," whispered Billy in a voice so low I could hardly hear him.

"What?" I asked as I watched him in the rear mirror, then made a fast turn onto our road.

"Saw bad man," Billy whispered.

"Are you sure?"

I pulled into the driveway; we all jumped out of the van and dashed up the steps. I didn't take another breath until we were safely in the house and the door locked securely behind us. I sat on the sofa and gathered my sons to me as we tried to calm our collective fears; Billy whimpered and clung to me while Johnny stared at the door as if he waited for the monster to find us. I almost screamed out loud when Mittens jumped onto the back of the sofa, startling me, then landed on Johnny's lap and stayed there. We stayed huddled together until Doug found us later that night.

Chapter 15

Mittens leapt onto the barstool next to me and butted his head against my thigh. He batted my arm with his paw as he tried to get my attention.

"Mroww," the cat emitted a plaintive sound.

I glanced down and rubbed his head absent-mindedly as my mind groped for answers. "I just don't know, Mittens. There must have been close to one hundred people there last night. It could be anyone."

My mind replayed all of our actions from the night before. We entered Wagner's, I signed the guest register; I greeted some folks from our church, ugh - those sickeningly sweet flowers... my brow creased in concentration as I tried to remember.

"Who could it be?" I stirred my now cold cup of coffee and stared into space, trying to visualize the scene again and what we were doing when Billy became frightened. I had spotted Anna and Chuck across the room talking with Martha Parker. I remember searching for Aunt Fran but didn't see her. "Oh dear, this is harder than I thought," I told Mittens.

Doug came downstairs with Billy and Johnny trailing behind him. The boys quietly ate their bowls of breakfast cereal; Johnny raised his eyes toward me and shook his head "no" to indicate that Billy had not spoken any more of the incident.

I folded two notes and handed one to each boy. I had scribbled a short excuse of fake tummy aches to explain their tardiness to school.

"Are you sure you want to go in today? If you don't feel comfortable, you can stay home with me. It's okay."

"Yeah, I want to go," Johnny said as he tucked his note into his coat pocket.

"I don't wanna miss Halloween, Mom. You always said if we were too sick to go to school, we were too sick to trick or treat," Billy explained with his child's reasoning.

I smiled for the first time that morning and embraced him in a tight hug. I tousled his hair, kissed him on the forehead, and pulled his jacket zipper up higher, then adjusted his collar.

"Daddy will drive you to school today and I'll pick you up. No school bus; look for our van when you get out."

"Okay," they both agreed as they trudged out the door.

Doug whispered in my ear as he gave me a quick kiss on the cheek, "They'll be fine. I'm gonna have a deputy patrol the school grounds during the day. How about you? Will you be okay?"

I sighed, "Yes, I've got things to do to prepare for Halloween and I may stop by Aunt Fran's. Better hurry, the boys will be late enough as it is."

"See you later," Doug said as he left the house.

Mittens gobbled his dish of canned cat food, a treat for him instead of the dry mix, then sauntered through his pet door to harass the unsuspecting birds outside. I watched him as I mechanically finished my housework chores, my mind churning on the puzzle of Fred Granger's murder.

Trick or treating and then the school's Halloween party would be later tonight. I poured three bags of candy bars and treats into a large plastic bowl in readiness for the little goblins ringing doorbells tonight and put aside another bag of candy to take to the school. Rummaging through the junk drawer in the laundry room cabinet, I got my hands on a pair of tea light candles that will do nicely inside Johnny's carved pumpkins. I clicked them on to check their batteries and decided they would be fine. I didn't want to worry about fire dangers with a real candle.

Upstairs, I discarded my robe and pajamas, then dressed in a pair of black corduroy slacks and a yellow turtleneck sweater. I slipped on knee socks but had to get down on hands and knees to search the back of my closet floor. Finally, I found the pair of short ankle boots I enjoy wearing in the winter. The leather was so pliant from years of wear; they felt like a soft glove as I zipped them up. I wanted an outfit that would be comfortable enough yet warm to wear during the day and get me through a cold evening of walking about the neighborhood with the kids.

Back downstairs, I checked on Mittens, then picked up my jacket and purse to head out. My destination... Aunt Fran's shop. I needed to talk to someone. I just couldn't cope with this by myself any longer.

I had expected downtown to be quiet this late in the morning; it was way after morning commute and too early for lunch, but I was surprised to see the number of cars lining both sides of Park and the crowd gathered outside the Knox Savings and Loan. I found an empty parking space a block away and was walking toward the dress shop when my aunt stepped outside. She had a watering can in her hand and was tending to the pots of mums sitting next to her door.

As I neared the shop, a funny feeling made me stop and look around. A strange man stood across the street; his hands cupped a meager flame as he attempted to light a cigarette, all the while his eyes stared at me. The hairs on the back of my neck prickled as I met his intense expression.

"Good morning," Aunt Fran greeted me with a smile.

I clutched her arm, spilling water from her sprinkler can, then pointed across the street to direct her attention. "Who is that man? Do you know him?"

Fran's gaze followed my direction, then shrugged as she turned back to me. "Who? I don't see anyone."

"Where'd he go? He was right there, staring at me; I could feel his eyes drilling holes right into the back of my head."

"That's strange. You better come into the shop," said Aunt Fran.

"I looked for you last night. Where were you?" I asked as I shut the door behind me and glanced around. The store was empty today; Betty had the day off and no customers. "I really need to talk to you."

"Let's get a cup of tea, I've got a kettle simmering in the back and we can sit down and chat."

"I can't talk to mom, she would just get all hysterical, but I really need to speak to someone. You've always been there for me, Aunt Fran. I don't know who else I can turn to," I cried as tears formed in my eyes. I sniffed and wiped them away with the back of my hand.

Aunt Fran gathered me in her arms and patted my back. She pulled back and held my face in her hands as she looked at me; a worried expression on her face.

"What's wrong? I'm here; you can talk to me about anything, you know that. Now tell me what has upset you. Is it Doug? Problems with the marriage?" she asked.

"What? No! Doug and I are good. No, it's this murder investigation that has me worried. I'm scared out of my mind."

"Why should you be scared? Oh dear, this is all my fault for insisting that you try to help Ted Williams. I should never have encouraged you to get involved."

"Well, I am involved now, and it's too late to turn back. If I tell you something, you must promise me to keep this secret."

"I promise," swore Aunt Fran; her brows lifted, causing worry lines across her forehead.

"Remember when I told you that Billy was having nightmares? Well, he finally told us that he saw the man who killed Fred Granger. The poor kid is scared silly. Now Doug worries that Billy might be in danger if the killer knew a witness could identify him," I cried.

137

"Oh my God. Who did he see?"

"I don't know. Billy couldn't tell us. The man must be a stranger to Billy. So, you see, this means I can prove Ted Williams is innocent. It must be someone from around town that Billy just hasn't met. What am I going to do?" I trembled at the thought of my child in danger.

Aunt Fran got up and began pacing back and forth across the room. She wrung her hands, clasping and unclasping them. "How long have you known this?" Her teeth nibbled at her bottom lip and the color of her face paled.

"Just a few days, then last night at the funeral home, Billy said he saw the bad man again. He was so upset he could hardly speak. The only thing I could think to do was leave immediately and get home," I explained.

"I didn't get to Wagner's until after eight o'clock. I had to make my night deposit for the store and lock up, so I was late. No wonder I didn't see you there; you must have already left."

"The place was packed. I saw Harry Logan and Sam Tilley; they were both in the crowd and Ted was there with Barb and their son Joey. I never did speak with Fred's children; I couldn't even approach where they were seated. We got to watch the military honor guard, that really impressed the boys, but then we ran out just before we approached the casket. At first, I thought the idea of seeing a coffin had upset Billy, but once we were outside, he told me he had seen the bad man again. That frightened all of us."

"And you have no idea of who Billy was looking at when..."

Shrill sirens screamed, and bright blue take-down lights shone through the storefront as several police cruisers filled the street. Aunt Fran and I rushed out the door to watch all the commotion. I spotted Doug marching into the savings and loan building accompanied by Sheriff Simmons. Other deputies performed crowd control of the disgruntled customers gathered in front of the building as they all attempted to push open glass doors to enter the bank lobby. Shouts of angry voices blended with sirens.

"Wow, what's going on over there?" I exclaimed.

"Those are some very unhappy people," stated Aunt Fran.

We watched as Doug and Sheriff Simmons strode out of the bank a few minutes later. I rushed across the street to speak with my husband before he got back into his cruiser.

"Hey, what's happening?" I asked him.

He turned to me, a frustrated expression on his face. "Not now, Merry. You see all these people? You caused this mob."

"Me?!"

"Yes, you and your snooping alerted all these folks to question their accounts and demand a reckoning from the bank."

"Isn't that a good thing? But what are you doing here? This crowd wasn't unruly until all the cop cars pulled in."

"We have a warrant to pick up Harry Logan and bring him in for questioning," Doug explained.

"For Fred Granger's murder?" I speculated.

"No, for embezzlement."

139

"Wow. So, where is he?" I asked as I looked around and didn't spot anyone sitting in the back of a patrol car.

"Looks like Fred skipped town. None of the bank employees have seen him since last night."

"He was at Wagner's last night. I saw him there. Do you think that's who Billy calls the bad man?"

"I doubt it. I can see Logan stealing money, but murder? Can't imagine him doing something violent," said Doug as he reached for his car door handle.

"Seems like quite a coincidence, if he's not," I muttered. I waited to cross the street as the police cars started pulling out. One car stayed behind with two deputies to calm the crowd of bank customers demanding to be heard.

Aunt Fran and I watched all the uproar for a few minutes, then went back into the store. A sip of my cup of cold tea made me shake my head.

"Yuck, need a warm-up?" I asked my aunt as I raised my cup and nodded toward hers. I walked into the back room and nuked my cup of tea in the microwave.

"No, I'm good. I've already had enough coffee and tea this morning, anyway."

"What a crazy morning," I said.

"So, what did Doug say? What's going on at the bank?" asked Fran.

"The sheriff has a warrant out for Harry Logan. He embezzled funds from the savings and loan. That's why all those homes are on a delinquent list and up for sheriff sale. Those poor people paid their mortgage payments with money in escrow that was supposed to go to the county for real estate taxes. Looks like Logan has been stealing for over a year and now that he was about to get caught, he skipped town. Doug says they'll have to put out one of those all points' bulletin for his capture."

"Oh, my goodness! I wonder what the bank will do to make it right with those customers. Obviously, they paid their taxes and the county really can't penalize them."

"Doug told me that mob out there was my fault," I giggled.

"Was he joking or serious? Just because you snooped into Fred's account and those others?" asked Aunt Fran.

"Yeah, something like that. All I did was make a few telephone calls to some bank customers whose names were on the sheriff sale. They have a right to know; don't you agree?"

"I believe you did the correct thing. Imagine having some deputy knock on your door and tell you to get out... it would be horrendous," Aunt Fran stated.

"Well, we aren't any closer to finding out who murdered Fred Granger, are we?" I asked as I plopped down on one of her short stools.

"Hmm, I suppose we have to cross Harry Logan off our list. Ted is safe; although, we knew all along that he was innocent, but now there's evidence to prove that... well, who's left?" asked Fran as she doodled with a pencil on the back of a packing slip.

"I'm still considering Sam Tilley. What kind of alibi does he have for that Sunday morning? I doubt he was in church," I remarked.

"Really, Merry, you can't be serious. Did I tell you he donated one hundred dollars to our food drive? Sam seems like such an affable gentleman, and I'm sure he would never do something so vicious."

"How can you be sure? He's still a stranger to most people and I know my Billy has never met him, so he could be the bad man that he saw. Affable, Aunt Fran? Really? I've only witnessed him be very disagreeable. Are we talking about the same man?"

"I just don't see your reasoning, but I'll be able to tell you more after Saturday night. I've got a dinner date with Sam," Fran announced.

"Aunt Fran! You can't do that. You might be putting yourself in danger. Suppose he's the one; wait until Doug can check him out," I begged, trying to reason with her common sense.

"Merry, I'm not getting any younger. He's a good-looking man, and he's asked me out to a nice dinner. That's all. I get lonely now and then. Try to understand," Aunt Fran spoke in a hushed voice.

"I'm sorry. I didn't think. You're always so busy with the shop and committees, I guess I thought your life was full. I'm so wrapped up in what Doug and the boys need, I didn't realize. I'm really sorry. But I still think you need to be on your guard."

"I will. I promise. If it makes you feel any better, I'll have a chat with Doug and let him know my plans and see what he says. Okay?" asked Fran.

"Okay," I agreed reluctantly.

Chapter 16

I left the dress shop when a few customers wandered in and then swung by Martha's to pick up a dozen donuts. Cinnamon sugar donuts and chilled apple cider would taste so yummy; I wanted to give the boys a special Halloween treat. I walked toward the bakery, with head down and eyes on the sidewalk; my mind reviewed the conversation with my aunt. Suddenly I bumped into a solid chest above a pair of long legs. Hands reached out to steady me as my balance teetered.

"Oh! I'm so sorry. I wasn't watching where I was going," I apologized as I raised my head to look at the man.

"No problem," he started to say then, "You! You're the reason I got pulled in for questioning by the cops. I told you before to stay out of my business!" Sam Tilley growled, a sneer curling his thin lips.

"But... but..." I stuttered. I was shocked at his vehement attitude and tone.

"Stay away from me, lady. You cause any more trouble for me, you'll wish you hadn't," he snarled and strode away, leaving me staring after him dumbstruck.

I stood on the sidewalk, frozen to the spot, unable to believe what just happened. I watched him walk two blocks, then climb into one of those big black Ram pickups. My composure rattled; I shook my head and continued toward Martha's when I spotted Doug in his cruiser. I waved to catch his attention, then ran toward him.

Breathless and panting, I rushed to my husband's side as he waited next to his car.

"What's wrong? Is it Billy?" he asked quickly.

"No, the boys are both fine. I just had a run in with Sam Tilley. Told me to stay out of his business or I'd be sorry. He practically threatened me!"

"Did he physically threaten you?" Doug inquired in a solemn voice. I saw him assess me with his eyes, reaching his own conclusions.

"He didn't touch me, but he was extremely angry. Kind of scared me."

Doug enfolded me within his strong arms and for the moment I felt secure again. I took a deep breath and exhaled slowly, then nodded. "What should I do?"

"Nothing. Stay away from him. Maybe now you'll listen to me when I tell you to stop this investigating," Doug insisted.

"You see now why I think he's a suspect? Innocent men don't fly off the handle like that. His temper just exploded," I cried.

"I'll make my own inquiries, but try to avoid him, that's all I can say. Where you off to now?" Doug asked.

"I planned on picking up some donuts at Martha's then stop by the school to check in with Colleen about the party. I have to pick up Billy and Johnny at three o'clock."

"Watch your back," he warned.

Children's laughter rang out from classrooms as I entered the side entrance of the brick school building. I smiled at the sight of gaily colored construction paper jack-o'-lanterns decorating the hallways. Looks like the students and teachers had been busy getting into the Halloween spirit. I proceeded to the principal's office located at the front of the school.

I rapped a quick knock as I opened the office door and grinned at my friend as she juggled a telephone in one hand and searched a stack of papers on top of the large desk with her other. Educational certificates and framed diplomas from the University of Michigan hung on the wall behind her. I glanced about and spied a sad-looking philodendron with wilted leaves hanging down from the edge of a corner file cabinet. Only Colleen managed to kill a houseplant like that. I had to chuckle to myself upon seeing the poor thing.

Colleen returned my smile and motioned me in as she returned to her harried caller.

"Mm-hmm, that's right. . .yes, I'm sure that will be fine, Mrs. Baker. Um, I'll see you there. Yes, thank you again," Colleen said politely as she hung up the telephone and breathed a sigh of relief.

"Everything okay?" I asked.

"That must have been the tenth parent calling to ask if the children will be safe at tonight's party. I've been fielding questions all day. I've also seen a sheriff deputy drive by our school several times; I don't know whether to feel more secure or worried."

"The parents' concern is understandable, I guess. Personally, I think the kids will be a lot safer in here than out on the streets trick or treating with a murderer still at large. Wonder if that mother thought of that," I said emphatically.

"I agree. What does Doug have to say about tonight? Are the police worried, is that why the extra patrols? Should I hire security, do you think?" Colleen asked, a flustered expression on her face as her phone rang shrilly again. She made a face at the offending object, then growled before reaching to answer it in her sweet, principal's voice.

I got up, gave her a thumbs up, and silently mouthed that I was going to the cafeteria. Closing her door silently behind me, I started down the hall toward the site of tonight's party to check on last minute preparations.

"Hello Mister Cooper, all ready for tonight's craziness?" I laughed as I greeted the janitor.

"How are you today, Merry? See you're in the thick of things as usual. Those little ones are so excited; they'll have so much fun tonight."

"I just thought I'd check on the party room decorations and food. Will you be here later too?"

"I will. I promised Miss Callahan that I'd help to set up the party and clean up later. My wife, Ida, loves to see the children in their costumes; she's coming along to lend a hand."

147

"Marvelous! I'll look forward to seeing her later. Do you know if Mrs. Williams is here yet?" I asked.

"I believe I saw her in the cafeteria. She's a hard worker, that one. Too bad about the trouble her husband's in," said Mr. Cooper.

"Hmm, well, thanks Mr. Cooper. See you later," I said and went in search of Barb.

I could hear Barb's voice speaking with someone as I pushed open the cafeteria door and met a droopy spider dangling in front of my face. Some of the decorations we hung yesterday needed reinforcements. I'll grab some tape and make the rounds and repairs. I pushed the fuzzy pipe cleaner creature out of my face and walked toward the kitchen.

As I entered the food prep area, I spied the back of a man leaving through the rear delivery door.

"Thanks again," called Barbara. She latched the door and turned, smiling when she saw me. "Hey, Merry!"

"Who was that?" I asked.

"Um, Sam Tilley."

"What was he doing here?"

"He dropped off twenty pounds of frankfurters for the party tonight. Wasn't that nice of him?"

"He did, huh? Why'd he do that?" I wondered.

"I dunno, maybe Colleen asked for a donation or something? The kids will love having hotdogs to eat along with the chips and sweet stuff, don't you think?"

"I'm sure the mothers will appreciate they'll be having more to eat than just junk," I commented. "So, what's left to do?" I looked at the trays of cookies, brownies and bags of potato chips lined up on the counters.

"Where do you want these?" Ted Williams asked as he struggled to carry a huge bushel basket filled with apples. He took a deep breath as he set his load down and straightened up.

"Hello, Ted. I didn't know you'd be here today," I said.

"Yeah, well, I don't exactly have much to do these days. Not too many people want to do business with someone arrested for murder. Besides, Barb needed a hand, and I wanted to help out," he explained.

"Well, it's good to see you." I glanced between him and Barb; her eyes glowed warmly when she looked at him, and there seemed to be an unspoken agreement and shared affection between them.

"Merry, can I talk to you for a moment?" Ted asked, gesturing for me to follow him.

"Sure. What's up?" We moved toward the far side of the room and pretended to inspect the window decorations.

"I wanted to thank you for helping me. Barb told me how you've been working to prove my innocence. It really means a lot to me; to have someone believe in me." Ted scrubbed his face with a hand that shook.

"I know you didn't kill Fred Granger, but think hard Ted, did you see anyone or hear anything right before I saw you?"

"I heard footsteps running, the cornstalks rustled loudly; that's why I pushed through the row of stalks to search, but then I thought maybe I was mistaken, and I only heard the scouts moving in the maze. I told the sheriff, but I'm not sure he believes me."

"Hmm, I don't think you were mistaken. Problem is, I'm at a loss as where to go now. I'm running out of ideas. We're missing something; I just don't know what," I said in frustration.

"Do you have anyone that you suspect?" Ted asked.

"Um, Sam Tilley for one. He and Fred argued, and Sam really does not have an alibi for that Sunday. I had my eye on Harry Logan from the bank, but now I'm pretty certain he's only guilty of theft. What do you think?"

"Yeah, I heard about the panic at the savings and loan. You sure stirred up a hornet's nest there," Ted chuckled.

"Hey, um, Barb appears happy. What's going on with you two? You can tell me it's none of my business, but she's my friend and I'd hate to see her hurt. Does she know about your, ah, lady friend over in Pottstown?"

"Barb and I had a long talk. She knows. My friend in Pottstown wants nothing to do with me; she even refused to talk to Simmons and verify we were together Saturday night. Guess she decided she better stay with her husband."

"Hmm, you know, Barbara has never wavered in her belief of your innocence. She's stood by you," I reminded him.

150

"I've been a fool. I admit it. Chalk it up to mid-life crisis or plain stupidity. Our divorce was a mistake; Barb never wanted it. We're going to try and get back together. I've got a lot of work to do mending relationships with my family."

"I'm happy to hear that. You know how fond I am of both of you. Maybe something good has come out of this mess after all."

Anna Thompson burst through the cafeteria doors with hands filled with trays of cupcakes as she announced her arrival to all with an exuberant hello. Ted and I immediately rushed to relieve her of her burdens.

"Hey, y'all, don't these look delicious?" Anna drawled.

"Hey, yourself," I said as I gave her a quick hug. We placed the cupcakes on the table and arranged a stack of napkins next to them.

"Everything looks great! The kids will love this. Oh my, just look at that basket of apples, reminds me of when we picked our own bushel at the orchard. We gonna have the kids dunk for those beauties or just eat 'em?" Anna asked.

"Guess we can do both," I suggested. "Where'd they come from, anyway?"

Ted spoke up as he balanced on a chair, trying to anchor my fuzzy spider onto his ceiling perch, "Some guy dropped them off. Not sure if he was from the Ross farm or Grangers."

"What did he look like?" I asked, chewing on my bottom lip.

"I don't know, average, I guess. Just some guy. He said he heard there was a party at the school and wanted to donate some apples. Seemed nice enough," Ted explained.

"Hmm, I wonder. . ."

Chapter 17

We finished organizing all the food trays for the party, then arranged the tables around the room perimeters to create a large open square of floor space where games could be played. Ted and Mister Cooper each took a handle of a large metal tub and hauled it into the center of the game space. Barb and I carried gallon jugs of lukewarm water to fill the tub, added a dozen apples and wrapped the base with a circle of towels. When the children bob for apples, hopefully the towels would keep the floor from becoming too wet.

A tall poster board held an outline of a skeleton; the blind-folded children will stick the cardboard bones in place with push pins. Colleen came up with this Halloween version of pin the tail on the donkey and laughed as she hung it and demonstrated the idea. The party committee also planned to award prizes for the best costumes, judged by a panel of three teachers following a parade of the children by various age groups.

"Looks good, everything should work," I proclaimed, then gathered up my handbag and said my farewells just as the bell rang to announce the end of the school day. I hurried outside to wait by our van and watched for Billy and Johnny.

"Mom! Look at my Halloween picture," exclaimed Billy, waving a gigantic piece of paper. "I drew a spaceman, just like me. See?" Silver glitter sparkled on the poster and floated into the air with each movement.

"My goodness, you certainly did. Nice job. Let's lay it in the back so that glitter doesn't coat everything. Okay?" I said as I opened the trunk hatch.

As soon as I popped the lid, I spied my backpack that I'd thrown into the corner of the trunk days ago. Suddenly, I remembered the items I had tucked into one of its pockets. I've got to give that key and scarf slide to Doug. I can't believe they completely slipped my mind. Shaking my head in disbelief, I added Billy's poster and closed the trunk.

The boys climbed into the rear seat and buckled up as I pulled away before the school buses got underway. Avoiding the delay of being behind bus constant stops, we made it home in only fifteen minutes. I grabbed my backpack, then carried in the bakery parcel and a gallon of fresh apple cider and placed them on the counter out of Mitten's reach. I tossed my backpack into the mud room until I had time to speak with my husband about my discoveries. I'm sure the scarf slide belonged to Ted and wouldn't be important now, but that key...

"Mmm, those look good. Can we have a donut before supper?" asked Johnny.

"You guys put your schoolbooks upstairs and wash up, then you can have a snack. We're just having grilled cheese sandwiches and bowls of chicken noodle soup tonight because there will be plenty to eat later at the party," I said.

"Can I put on my spaceman suit?" Billy called down from upstairs.

"How about you wait until after supper? You don't want to spill soup on it," I suggested.

"Oh, okay," he agreed grudgingly as he tromped back into the kitchen and hopped up onto a bar stool.

I poured two small glasses of apple cider for Billy and Johnny and placed the cinnamon donuts on two paper plates. I decided I might as well enjoy one too, as I took a bite of the sweet treat.

"Mmm... these are so good," I murmured, chewing appreciatively. I grabbed a couple cans of soup from the pantry and placed a saucepan on the stove. "Johnny, when you're done with that, how about setting the table for me? Just lay out some spoons and napkins at each place setting. I'll keep plates and bowls here."

"Okay, Mom."

"Thanks buddy. Do you have your costume all set for tonight? Need any help with that green face paint for your zombie?"

"Yeah, maybe. I thought I would just smear on some goo. Zombies are supposed to look yucky," Johnny declared.

"You're right. We'll see what we can do later," I said as I tousled his hair. "Hey, maybe I can put some gel in your hair to make it stick up too. What d'ya think?"

Doug got home early so he could see the boys before they went out trick or treating. I noticed he didn't remove his deputy belt or change out of his uniform. I raised an eyebrow and gave him a

155

questioning look, but he just shrugged his shoulders to indicate he'd tell me later.

I prepared dinner quickly, serving the sandwiches and bowls of soup while the boys chatted excitedly. They were both so eager to dress in their costumes and get outside. Halloween thrills overrode their previous worries and made them forget their fear of the *bad man*. But not me. Fred's murderer was never far from my mind, especially tonight when everyone hid behind a mask and anyone could be a threat.

Doug laughed with the boys' antics then glanced at my face, reading my mind and acknowledged my concerns.

"Now listen guys, your mother and I want you to have fun tonight, but you've got to promise me you will obey my rules. First of all, stay within sight of your mom at all times, understand? Limit your trick or treating this year to just our neighborhood; our block and the two intersecting streets. Only knock on houses of people we know. You can enjoy plenty of candy once you get to the school party. Promise me?" Doug spoke to each of our sons in a quiet but firm voice.

They both nodded solemnly. "Yes, sir."

"Good. All the deputies in my office are on patrol tonight, including me. I want you to feel safe, but I also don't want you taking any chances. Got it?" Doug said as he looked from boy to boy and then me.

156

"Will we see you later at the school party?" I asked him as he reached for his cap and prepared to leave. "I've got something to show you," I said, thinking of that unusual key.

"Save it, don't have time now; I've got to run. I'll try to swing by the party later; it ends at nine o'clock. Right?"

"Yes. I may stay a bit longer to help Mister Cooper clean up; probably Barb or Anna will lend a hand too. Want me to save a hotdog for you?" I asked as I walked him to the door.

"No, don't bother. Just be careful. Remember what we're dealing with – there's still some lunatic liable to be walking around out there tonight," Doug cautioned again as he gave me a quick peck on the cheek and left.

With that sobering thought, I planned some precautions of my own and loaded up my heavy coat pockets with a short flashlight, a loud dog whistle, my cell phone, and a can of pepper spray. If anyone tries to sneak up on me, I swear they'll regret it because I intended to zap them. On impulse, I added the key to my pants' pocket as well. I wanted to show it to Anna or maybe Aunt Fran and see what they make of its odd design.

The boys ran upstairs to dress as I cleaned up the kitchen. Both of them nearly trampled Mittens as they vaulted down the steps in their haste to model their costumes in front of me. I smeared zombie green and gray colored crayon makeup onto Johnny's face, then spread a liberal glob of hair gel to spike his brown hair. He insisted on adding some drops of red raspberry jam to simulate congealed blood on his

157

neck. I cringed seeing that sticky stuff on his skin; yuck, I wouldn't be able to stand it.

Billy decided to wear Johnny's football helmet now that we had covered it with aluminum foil. I still needed to attach the silver pipe cleaner antennae onto the top of the helmet for effect.

"Billy, try to stand still for five minutes," I commanded, exasperated, as I attempted to staple the end of the antennae to the foil once again. The helmet face guard would hide part of his face from view so he wouldn't need any other mask for disguise. Billy twisted and turned as he tried to see himself in the hallway mirror.

"This rocket looks really cool, Mom," Billy said as he pointed to the applique I had stitched onto the chest.

"Glad you like it." The silver lamé fabric of his space suit sparkled under the kitchen's fluorescent lights. *"Costume turned out pretty well, if I say so myself,"* I thought as I admired my handiwork.

"Hope you're both dressed in something warm under those things. Okay, guys, just give me five more minutes and I'll be ready to go."

I grabbed a large black marker and a piece of yellow construction paper for a sign. Using the marker, I drew wide letters that read "Please Take One". I placed the bowl of Halloween candy and treats outside on my top step then propped up the sign behind it. A piece of tape anchored the sign against the door so it wouldn't blow away. I switched on our outside lights, illuminating the rear kitchen entrance as well as the front door and steps. Now I could accompany the boys for trick

158

or treating and not feel guilty by cheating the children who would stop by our house. The only thing left to do was light the candles in our pumpkins with a flick of the switch. The tiny battery-operated tea lights glowed a soft yellow through the pumpkin's carved eyes.

A full harvest moon drifted across the inky sky, then hid behind murky gray clouds only to emerge again to bathe little ghouls and goblins in silvery moonlight as they skipped along the city streets. Wind blew, scattering autumn leaves and whipped branches with gusts of chilled air foretelling a colder winter ahead. I drew the collar of my coat closer against my neck to ward off the brisk air.

I watched my sons as they visited our neighbors' homes, begging for treats and thanking them politely before jumping off porch steps or running across lawns to quickly knock on the next door. I waved and greeted folks as I hung back and waited on the sidewalk while the boys made their rounds.

Stately older homes lined the street, a few were graced with wide stoops or sweeping wrap-around front porches. Most of the neighbors decorated for the holiday with pumpkins, mums, or shocks of dried corn. We approached one Victorian home sparsely lit by a shallow yellow light above their door, the porch cast in deep recesses. As we neared the house, I spotted a lone figure standing in the corner. I paused and placed a hand on Billy's arm to stop him from going further. Johnny ran ahead before I could stop him and pressed the doorbell button. The portal opened, flooding the porch in light, and illuminated my suspicious character – a scarecrow.

"Oh, my goodness," I mumbled, feeling ridiculous as we left for the next house.

I watched as a small group of younger children were accompanied by mothers and baby strollers; they made their way up Maple drive at a much slower pace, but with an equal amount of glee. One little girl looked so cute in her *Little Red Riding Hood* outfit and even carried a basket to hold her candy treats. Her brother hurried after her, dressed in a wolf costume; obviously coordinated by their mother, who was thinking of the school costume prizes to come later in the evening.

We made our way down Maple, then turned the corner onto Oak with a stop at the Thompson home. Anna sat on her front steps, wrapped in a large quilt, and handed out candy to the children as we approached.

"Howdy! You boys having a good time? Stevie is across the street; he's wearing a cowboy rig. You'll spot him, he's the Lone Ranger."

Billy and Johnny each thanked Anna for the couple of candy bars she tossed into their goody bags, then dashed across the street to find Stevie and visit a few more houses.

"What time are you going to the school party?" I asked Anna.

"I'm allowing Stevie to trick or treat another half hour before we head over. How 'bout you?"

"Probably the same. We promised Doug we would limit our visits to just these streets and folks we know," I said as I took a seat on her bottom step and kept the boys in sight.

"Hmm, know what you mean. Is the sheriff any closer to arresting somebody?" asked Anna.

"I really don't know. I wish I did. Oh, hey, check out this key I found in the corn maze last Monday. I dug it out of the dirt when I picked up my backpack, then completely forgot about it. What do you think it opens?" I pulled the key from my pocket and laid it into my friend's palm.

Anna turned the key over and over, held it up to her bright coach lamp to study its markings. She scratched off a bit of dirt clinging to the etched patterns and grooves.

"You found this in the maze? Looks like one of those bank keys for safe deposit boxes, or maybe something that opens an antique chest. I've got an antique steamer trunk; it has a fancy key like this," Anna suggested.

"I thought it strange, finding it there of all places. Don't know whether Fred dropped it, or it could have been buried in that land for years and just got churned up when the corn crop was planted. I don't even know if it's important, just weird," I said as I shoved the key back into my pocket.

"Here come the kids," Anna said as she pointed to the group.

"We'll do one more street, then head over to the school," I told the boys as I got up to walk with them to the next block. "See you at the party," I called out to Anna.

The dense canopy of trees that lined both Oak and Elm streets blocked moonlight and street lamps as we made our way toward the

161

last group of homes. Twice I stopped in my tracks and peered into the darkness, thinking I had seen some movement behind a shrub or in a side yard. *"My nerves must be getting to me,"* I thought, as I tried to shake off a feeling of unease that I could not explain.

"You guys done?" I called out to Billy and Johnny as they walked toward me. "Let's get home and put your bags inside, then we can go to the party."

"Okay Mom," Billy agreed as he and Johnny walked with me the two blocks back to our house.

I checked on our candy bowl sitting on the front step, it still had some contents left so I left it out for any late stragglers. Our pumpkins continued to glow cheerfully to greet any trick or treaters.

Unlocking the kitchen door, we entered the house. The boys dumped their treat bags onto the countertop, then ran upstairs for a fast bathroom break.

"Mroww," Mittens loudly reminded me that his water bowl was empty and that he needed to be fed.

"Okay, I hear you. Just a minute fella," I told him as I rubbed his arched back and knuckled the top of his head. Mittens purred, then walked in and out between my legs as he followed my every step from the storage cabinet with his pet food to his bowls.

Pit stop completed, I turned a lamp on in the living room and left a night light burning in the kitchen as I locked up behind us and we climbed into our van. I slowly backed out of the driveway and turned when my headlights partially caught a figure hiding in the shadows of the corn field behind our house.   He ducked quickly back into obscurity as the arc of my headlights moved. I paused and stared into the night, not sure if my imagination had played a trick on me or if I really did see someone there.

"What's wrong, Mom?" Johnny questioned nervously, as he watched me peering into the dark.

"Hmm? Nothing. Thought I saw something, but I was wrong. Let's go," I said as I put the van in gear and pulled away.

Chapter 18

Balloons of varying sizes in gay orange and yellow colors swayed in the night air; their long string tails tied firmly to the Meadowood School fence posts. Colleen had also attached a long banner above the front entrance to announce the Halloween party. Decorated pumpkins marched up the concrete steps leading to the main door. Cars filled the school parking lot and lined the street on both sides for two blocks. The community had turned out for the big event.

Laughter and gaiety bubbled over as both children and adults arrived. Delicious aromas of grilled hotdogs teased nostrils of hungry party goers entering the event room. Lines of people approached the food tables, filling plates with candy treats, pretzels or chips, cupcakes and cookies cut in fun shapes of pumpkins, witches or black cats. Cups of Hawaiian punch and bottles of water helped quench thirsts. I glanced about the room, taking it all in.

"Go ahead, you guys help yourself to some sweets and be sure and get a hotdog too," I told Billy and Johnny as they scampered off.

I elbowed my way through the crowd and entered the kitchen area, then slipped off my coat and hung it on a hook in exchange for one of the school aprons. Wrapping the long apron ties about my waist, I crisscrossed the strings in the back and tied a small bow in front. Barb Williams stood before the steamy grill surface, turning over frankfurters and transferring cooked ones onto large oval platters.

"Hey Barb, what can I do to help? Need a break? I can take over here," I offered as I picked up a pair of long tongs.

"Thanks, Merry. We've been swamped; I think everyone came at the same time. Can you open some more bags of buns? They're over there."

"Sure, no problem. Party looks like it's a big hit," I said.

"We've had a good turn out."

"Is Ted here?" I asked as I took over grill duties and Barb started serving a dog in a bun to a pair of waiting princesses.

"Yes, he's helping out with some of the games. He dressed in his scout uniform as a costume," Barbara commented with a chuckle.

I looked down at my own clothes, "Guess you could say I'm a bumblebee with my black pants and yellow sweater. I never even thought of a costume for myself," I snorted in a short laugh.

"Several of the parents really got creative in their costumes though," Barb said as she pointed out three werewolves, two evil witches and a Dracula or two moving about the room.

"I see what you mean; look at that guy, he really looks amazing as the Phantom of the Opera. Unique costume; wonder who he is," I said as I studied the man's size and height. As I stared at him, I realized that the eyes behind his mask appeared to be staring right back at me. How unnerving! I quickly broke eye contact and looked down at the grill and my task at hand.

165

People crowded into the cafeteria space and overflowed into the hallway. The din of voices talking and laughing, children squealing, and shouting thundered inside the school building. The school principal, Colleen Callahan, picked up a portable microphone and stood before the kitchen doorway. She waved her hand as she tried to gain everyone's attention.

Finally, the level of noise in the room lessened as people shuffled toward their host. Colleen waved again, then spoke into the mike, "Hello! Welcome to Meadowood's first annual Halloween party. Thank you all for coming. Is everyone having a good time?"

For her answer, applause and cheers rang out along with the thunder of stamping feet. Smiles shown on everyone's face.

"Great! We want to ask the children to do a little parade for the judges so if everyone would please step back and clear a space in the center of the room, we can begin our contest," Colleen directed. Adults shifted about and moved toward the perimeters of the room to form an open aisle leading from the doorway into the center game area.

Anna Thompson stepped forward to help organize the children into age groups, with the younger children going first. Giggling five, six-and seven-year-olds tried to form a line but could hardly stand still. The older children began assembling in the hallway as they prepared march in.

"Our judges tonight are fourth grade's Miss Jamison, Mrs. Klausson from our kindergarten, and Mister Housewright, our second-grade teacher. Prizes will be awarded for the most original costume,

166

scariest, and the prettiest." Colleen clapped her hands and signaled Anna to start the parade of young children.

A ballerina skipped past the panel of judges followed by a good witch with her magic wand, a tiny wicked witch holding a broom, and two princesses wearing pink tulle gowns and sparkling tiaras in their hair. Pastel pink or blue satin half masks covered their eyes and nose, but not the broad smiles on their faces. Next came a Stars Wars storm trooper, a combat soldier dressed in camouflage with his arm in a sling, a pair of clowns, and a short Dracula. Little Red Riding Hood ran into the room chased by her brother dressed as the Big Bad Wolf. Parents watching broke out into laughter at their antics. All the children giggled and spun about as they modeled their outfits; they looked so cute. It would be difficult to select a winner.

Next came the older children, mostly boys, as they jostled for positions and marched into the room. Billy proudly wore his spacesuit and helmet; the antennae jiggled as he moved his head. Stevie Thompson appeared every inch the Lone Ranger with his black cloth mask, Stetson hat and cowboy outfit. Johnny stood among a number of zombies; grouped together like they had just left the cast of the *Walking Dead*. One kid was especially gruesome in his zombie makeup, applied much more professionally than Johnny's. They were an impressive lot.

Everyone clapped and gave a final round of applause for all the contestants. The judges put their heads together and quietly discussed their choices, then nodded to Colleen as she received their tally.

167

"The winners are..." Colleen began her announcement. The room hushed in anticipation, "The prettiest is Sally Gibson as Princess Aurora, Todd Wilson's zombie wins the scariest costume and it seems we have a tie vote on most original. Susie and Byron Wise as Little Red Riding Hood and the Wolf made a very original duo plus Billy Gardner in his outer space alien costume. Congratulations everyone! The winners will all receive a gift card to McDonald's. All participants will also receive a special treat bag of goodies.

"Hooray!" I cheered and applauded loudly as Billy clasped his gift card prize and ran toward me.

"I won!" he exclaimed as I enveloped him in a bear hug.

"I know. Well done," I said, so proud of him.

I looked up from my son's smiling face as I felt a wariness and prickling on the back of my neck. Oddly, the Phantom of the Opera had sidled closer to us. Who was that guy? He was obviously staring at Billy and me in an ominous manner. Was it my imagination or just the creepy mask and costume that conveyed that impression?

"Come on Billy, let's grab some chips and a hotdog then find a place to sit down. Want a cup of Hawaiian punch or a bottle of water?" I asked as I hurriedly pulled him along behind me. The Phantom stayed where he was, but I was certain his eyes followed us.

We found a couple of empty chairs at a side table where we joined Anna and Aunt Fran. I had continued to keep a watchful eye for the Phantom while I ate, but he had disappeared in the crowd. I kept recalling that weird prickling sense and fear that I felt earlier when we were trick or treating and related it to what I had experienced now.

"Congratulations Billy!" Aunt Fran pressed a kiss to his cheek as he squirmed in his chair.

"Aww, geez Aunt Fran," Billy complained about his aunt's mushy show of affection as he scrubbed his wet cheek.

"Yes sir, mister spaceman. Your wish is my command," she joked and mussed his hair. Fran moved his helmet off another chair and sat down. "Do you mind?"

Billy finished his hotdog, gulped down a cup of punch, then jumped up. "I'm gonna get a cupcake," he said as he ran across the room toward his goal. Anna took his vacated seat.

"Wow, what a turn out," said Aunt Fran as she pointed to the crowd moving about the room.

"Yeah. Colleen's party is a hit," I agreed. "Glad you came, Aunt Fran."

"How's everything been going? You and the boys okay?"

"We're fine. I can't say that the day hasn't been without its moments, though."

"What do you mean?"

"You ever get a feeling like you're being watched or just a sense that you're in danger? We went trick or treating in the neighborhood and twice I had that weird feeling of being watched, then I thought I saw someone in the dark behind our house. Then here tonight... I

169

can't put my finger on it," I tried to keep my voice low and not draw attention among the group of people crowded near us.

"Do you think someone is following you? The man that Billy saw?" whispered Aunt Fran.

"I don't know, God, I hope not! I've been meaning to ask you, what do you think about this?" I asked as I pulled the mysterious key out of my pants pocket.

Aunt Fran fingered the embossed key and studied it in the palm of her hand. "Where did you get this?"

"I found it at the corn maze when I went back for my bag Monday morning. It was in the dirt near the spot where Fred died. I put it away and forgot about it until this afternoon. Do you think it opens a bank box or something? That's what Anna thought."

"Maybe it's for an antique chest," suggested Anna as she watched Fran try to read the key's engraving.

"I don't think so. I'm not certain, but this looks like one of the safe deposit box keys that Wells Fargo issued when they first opened their branch in Meadowood. Gosh, must have been at least forty years ago. I have a box there, but my key looks different from this. However, I remember seeing the manager with a fancy key like this on display. Commemorative or something for the bank," Aunt Fran explained.

"Hmm, that's interesting. How did it get buried in a cornfield?" asked Anna.

"Don't know. Guess I'll turn it over to Doug and Sheriff Simmons tomorrow," I said as I slipped it back into my pants pocket.

"Time to get these young'uns organized or they'll be running all over the place like jack rabbits," drawled Anna as she got up to start the games.

"Guess I better get back to the kitchen too and take my turn cooking," I said as I cleared our paper plates and cups and carried them to a tall trash barrel.

"I'll help," volunteered Aunt Fran.

I shooed Barb out of the kitchen for a much-needed break and took over the grill again. Aunt Fran washed off a group of apples and arranged them attractively in a basket on one of the treat tables.

"Have you seen Sam roaming about?" asked Fran as she returned to the kitchen work area.

"He was here earlier today when he dropped off these hotdogs, but I haven't seen him since. Unless... he's in costume and I just don't recognize him. Why?"

Aunt Fran gave me an exaggerated look and snorted, "Just asking, that's all. I was hoping I'd see him. I really do think you're wrong about that man."

"Well, for your sake, I hope I am. As strange as that man is, though, I really doubt he would show up at a kids' Halloween party. Can you just imagine him dressed in a costume? Or maybe he is..." I murmured, my voice falling off to a whisper, as my eyes scanned the room.

"What? Do you see him?" Aunt Fran craned her neck to study the crowd.

171

"Check out the guy dressed as the Phantom of the Opera. Could that be Tilley? I caught him staring at me twice." I pointed to the mysterious man trapped in a corner and surrounded by screaming children waiting to bob for apples.

Fran followed my gaze and tipped her head to one side as she considered the man's size and height.

"I'm not sure. Could be. The height's about right. I think he would have told me if he intended to dress for the party. I know I made a point of telling him that I'd be here tonight," said Aunt Fran.

"Sounds like you're getting close to that man."

"Well, we met for coffee after work the other day, and he did ask me out on a real dinner date for tomorrow night. I may have spoken to him on the phone once or twice, but that's all." Aunt Fran smiled in a dreamy way, her thoughts elsewhere.

"Holy cow! I thought you only spoke to him that one day in his shop. Did you talk to Doug about him, like you promised?" I asked.

"No, but I will. I told you I would. I've just been too busy with the shop this week and Halloween plus the food drive. You know how it is," Aunt Fran defended herself.

Chapter 19

I kept watching both the clock and the door, waiting on Doug to arrive while becoming more and more disappointed as the evening wore on and the hands on the clock pointed toward nine. His absence puzzled me. The kitchen had finally run out of hotdogs; we'd consumed all twenty pounds, and the cupcake and cookie trays were becoming bare. The party was definitely winding down.

The children had loved playing the skeleton game and squealed in delight at bobbing for apples. Poor Mister Cooper twice had to mop the floor surrounding the apple tub due to all the sloshing water. Now, as I looked around the room, all I saw were lots of tired children and worn out parents.

Several families prepared to leave and call it a night. Masks hung down around ears and costumes drooped, now face makeup smeared or was removed as Halloween wound to an end until another year.

"Can I help scrub that grill for you gals while you clean up the kitchen counters?" asked Ida Cooper.

"Thank you, Mrs. Cooper, that's kind of you to offer," I said as Anna and I stuffed soiled paper plates and cups into a large black trash bag.

Colleen and Barb Williams worked to consolidate the trays of baked goods onto one platter while we gathered up the remaining debris. Ted and Mister Cooper began arranging tables and chairs back into the cafeteria's normal layout.

"Mom, can I go home with Joey tonight? His mom said it's okay. He invited me to sleep over," Johnny begged, his expression hopeful.

"Well, I suppose so. I'll drop off some decent clothes for you to wear tomorrow morning; can't have you dressed like a zombie," I told him. I smiled at his exuberance.

"Yay! Thanks, Mom," Johnny cheered as he ran over to his friend.

"Barb, you sure it won't be any problem having Johnny go home with you?" I asked as Barb and Ted grabbed their coats from the kitchen coat rack.

"No problem. The boys are still wound up; Ted promised to show them a spooky Halloween movie, and I said I'd cook a bowl of buttered popcorn for them. Johnny can wear a pair of Joey's pj's tonight."

"Okay. I'll swing by in the morning and bring him some clothes when I pick him up. Ten o'clock okay?" I asked.

"Fine. See you then," Barb said as she and Ted with the two boys left by the side door.

Anna and Ida scooped out the remaining apples from the barrel while Mister Cooper walked down the hall to grab his mop and bucket before emptying the tub of water.

"Billy— let's get ready to go," I said as I slipped on my coat and glanced around the room. "Thanks for all of your help, Anna."

"No problem. I'll call you tomorrow," Anna shouted as she and her son opened the rear door to leave.

Ida slipped on her coat, preparing to leave too. "I need to sit down; my knees ache. Tell Joe I'm waiting in the car."

"Okay. He ought to be right back," I replied, holding Billy's helmet in my left hand. I rocked on the balls of my feet, stretching as I waited; my right hand tucked in my pocket, jiggled the contents as my fingers fondled the various objects.

"I gotta use the bathroom," hollered Billy as he dashed down the hallway toward the restrooms.

"Don't be too long," I called after him.

Suddenly ceiling lights clicked off, thrusting the cafeteria into deep shadows; only dim amber lamps glowed above the door exit signs. I stood in the center of the room waiting on Billy as my eyes tried to adapt in the pitch-darkness.

"Mister Cooper must have assumed everyone had gone home and switched off the lights," I thought to myself. Hearing footsteps, I turned toward the sound, my eyes strained to see in the blackness. Hairs on the back of my neck raised, a warning tingling pricked my skin.

"Billy, is that you? C'mon let's go."

"I want that key," a deep menacing voice spoke in the shadows.

"What? Who are you?" I demanded, in a trembling voice; I hated myself for showing fear as his footsteps came closer.

I could barely discern the outline of the Phantom, his black silhouette framed against the hallway entrance. A shorter shadow

175

blotted out the faint glimmer of light behind him and I immediately recognized it as my son, Billy. I heard Billy gasp as the man ripped off his mask and tossed it away. He turned to face my son then returned his focus on me.

The Phantom moved toward me. My only thought was to flee. I took a step backwards; my foot bumped into the edge of the tin tub. I quickly bent and tipped the tub; water spilled onto the vinyl flooring and soaked the man's feet. I wildly threw the helmet at him but missed my target.

"Run, Billy, run!" I shouted as I sprinted to my right and knocked the Phantom backwards. He slipped on the wet floor and tried to gain his footing but went down on one knee. I felt his hand reach out and grab the hem of my coat. My fingers closed on the can of pepper spray in my pocket; I pulled it out and aimed at the vague shape. He yelped; his hands clawed the space between us. I took advantage of the moment to yank my coat free from his grasp and run toward the hall.

I sprinted down the vacant hallway with a speed a high school track star would envy. I caught up to Billy and grabbed his hand, pulling him along with me. We pushed against one of the classroom doors; no good, it was locked tight. Hearing a growl and movement behind us, I quickly headed for the basement as we took the stair steps two at a time.

We leaped into the lower corridor and almost tripped over the prone body of Joseph Cooper. The poor janitor lay unconscious,

176

bleeding from a cut on his head. His mop and bucket dropped, lay haphazardly across the entrance to the maintenance room.

Flashback memories of being trapped in this basement as a child came rushing back to me as I negotiated the maze of corridors seeking a place to hide. I reached for the cell phone in my pocket. I needed to call for help but was also afraid that the lit screen would give away our position. I risked a quick glance as I pressed the on button; just as I feared, no signal down here with so many iron pipes and ducts.

Billy and I crept forward past the electrical room with its wall of circuit breakers and emergency generators, then entered the furnace room. The old coal furnace with its wide octopus-like duct work had been replaced years ago with a more modern gas furnace and hot water boiler to feed warm radiators, but the original coal chute and storage bin were still in place against the far wall. We crawled into the open bin to hide while I tried to judge the width of the blackened chute and its trap door set into the wall above it. I stared at the ancient ramp as a plan percolated in my mind.

"I'm scared. Will the bad man find us?" cried Billy. Tears flowed and created black streaks down sooty cheeks covered in coal dust.

"Shh, don't be afraid. Everything will be all right. See that little door up there?" I pointed above the coal chute. "Do you think you can crawl up this ramp and push open the flap? Mommy needs you to go get help. Can you do that?" I whispered as I held him to me.

Billy hiccupped; his eyes wide as saucers as he looked at the door high above. He shook his head no and trembled, then huddled closer to me. I knew he was frightened, but it was our only way out or we'd be trapped here waiting until the murderer found us.

"You can do this Billy. Mommy needs you to be brave now. Pretend it's a game; just crawl up that chute. See, it looks just like the playground sliding board. Push open the door on the top and you'll be right outside. Here, take my cell phone and call 911 when you get outside. Call your daddy."

He gulped and clung to me once more before he nodded, then shoved the phone into his pocket and started to crawl slowly upward on the black slide. His once shiny silver space suit rapidly became coated in decades' old coal dust. Billy grasped the edge of the trap door and yanked, but nothing happened; the door stayed stuck shut. The effort made him skid downwards on the chute before he could brake himself, then crawled back to the top.

"Try again," I whispered in as loud a voice as I dared. "Pull hard!"

"Okay."

I watched Billy brace himself with his rubber soled sneakers against each side of the chute and grabbed the door handle with both hands. He pulled hard and the door creaked open. The flap raised, accompanied by a rush of chilly air that swept over us. Billy thrust his head through the open door, his slender shoulders and body followed in the narrow opening then into the freedom of the night. The trap door slammed shut behind him.

"Thank God. He's safe now," I prayed as I watched my son escape. Now all I needed to do was wait for the cavalry to come to my rescue. Unfortunately, my Phantom had other ideas.

Chapter 20

The school was as silent as a graveyard. I held my breath as my own heart pounded so loudly in my chest, I was certain it echoed within the dark basement. I strained to hear the slightest sound that would reveal the location of my stalker. Did he double back? Could Billy be in danger of being found outdoors? Peering into the blackness, I slowly moved from my spot in the furnace room as I retraced my steps toward the staircase and escape.

I felt like a child again, alone within the school's black caverns surrounded by mysterious and scary shapes. I swallowed and tried to calm my nerves. Nothing had happened to me then, and nothing will happen now. My imagination was my worst enemy, and I must not let it get the best of me now. Who was I kidding?

"Hmm, tell that to the crazy guy hunting me," I whispered into the stillness.

I crept behind a stack of boxes, then waited for my heart rate to slow as I took a deep breath. My eyes strained to see as scant sounds of rustling fabric and soft footsteps reached my ears. He was coming.

I crawled forward into what appeared to be a storage room. Boxes of paper were stacked four feet high, cases of crayons and pencils sat on metal shelving units - all the normal school supplies. Rolls of paper towels, packages of toilet paper, and bottles of liquid soap filled the sagging shelves. I tried to hide in the windowless room, finding meager comfort in one of its obscure corners. I pulled my woolen coat tighter across my chest to cover my yellow sweater that shown like a beacon in the night.

A cruel laugh bounced off the stone walls. I cringed as his voice rang out, "You can't get away from me. There's no way out."

I cowered in silence, praying he could not hear my heavy breathing. *"Oh God, what's taking Doug so long? He should be here by now."* My thoughts screamed in my mind.

The minute sliver of light suddenly vanished, blocked by the figure filling the doorway. I crouched low, hoping he would not spot me. I could see him stand there and hesitate, as if he were trying to decide whether to enter or move on in his search. I held my breath again as I watched the menacing silhouette. I must have made some small noise as he quickly pivoted his head to listen then stepped into the storage room.

"Give me that key. I promise I won't hurt you," he called out.

I debated on whether or not to answer him. I cowered in the dark, trying to summon my courage. Finally, I decided that I could not wait for him to find me and just take what he wanted; I had to do something.

"I don't believe you. Who are you? What's so important about an old key?" I asked as I stood up but remained in the shadows. I frantically searched about for some kind of weapon to use against him if he came closer.

"You don't need to know," he snarled.

181

"Tell me your name; I'll decide if you get the key," I urged him.

"You don't make the rules here, lady. I do. I'll hand it to you though, most women would be sniveling in tears by now." He snorted in a half laugh that finished in a sneer. He took a step forward.

The concrete basement floor had cracked over the years, and the surface sloped downward. As I had crouched low behind the flimsy metal shelving, I noticed one leg had been shimmed with a thin piece of wood to correct the balance of the unit on the uneven floor. With no time to spare, I pushed with all my strength against the metal shelving unit to pitch it forward. Gravity took over as boxes and materials flew and the metal frame crashed against the Phantom, trapping him beneath it.

I jumped over the scattered boxes and ran for the door. He growled and cursed behind me; I heard him toss the empty shelving aside as he crawled out. I dashed toward the electrical room and the fire alarm switch I recalled seeing outside its door. I reached for the handle and pulled it downward; shrill alarm bells rang, a recorded message announced the building evacuation, while red flashing lights became activated in the passageway leading to the stairwell. The change from complete blackness to bright strobe lights blinded me.

I stumbled as I rushed toward the steps. Mister Cooper moaned and tried to sit up as I went to his aid. I could hear sirens outside approaching the school. The police might be slow in coming to our rescue, but I knew the fire station would immediately dispatch to an alarm from the school.

I turned and glared at the man bearing down on us. A look of pure rage emanated from his piercing eyes, now void of any mask.

Before he could advance any closer, I grabbed the discarded long-handled rag mop and swung it at him like a warrior with a broad sword. It smacked him across the face; dirty water dripped from his chin. I drew back the mop and thrust it again like a ram rod straight into his chest, knocking him backwards off his feet. I stood looking down at him and continued to press the mop head into his chest to hold him in place as shouts rang out in the floors above us.

I gripped my dog whistle in my mouth and blew as loudly as I could. The piercing sound announced our location to the team of firemen in full regalia and sheriff deputies with guns drawn as they descended upon us.

Paramedics quickly attended to Joseph Cooper while the fire chief turned off the blaring alarm to permit us all to hear normally again. Two deputies relieved me of my prisoner as they hauled him to his feet and placed handcuffs on his wrists.

Doug hurried to my side and wrapped his arms about me.

"Are you okay? What in the world were you thinking?"

"Where's Billy? Is he safe?" I asked worriedly. "Did he call you?"

"I got some kind of crazy call from him and an older woman named Ida. All Billy could tell me was that the bad man had chased you inside the school. Poor little guy was crying so hard, I could hardly understand him. He's waiting with Ida in her car."

183

I stared at the man standing in the tatters of a wet Phantom of the Opera costume. He glared at me as I demanded again, "Who are you?"

"Allen Granger," he spat.

"Granger? You killed your own father?! Why?" I queried in disbelief.

"I must caution you of your Miranda rights," the Sheriff began, and proceeded to inform Allen Granger of his right to remain silent and his right to an attorney. "You understand that anything you say can be held against you in a court of law?" continued Simmons.

"Yeah, yeah. I didn't mean to kill him; stupid old man was just so damned stubborn. If he'd just listened to reason, we could have made a lot of money on that dumb farm. I wanted to drill for gas, but no, he wouldn't allow it. Said he would not stand by and have fracking disturb the environment," Allen fumed.

"Then what happened?" prompted Doug.

"We were walking along the cornfield, he wanted to check on the maze. I don't know, I just lost my temper when he told me he had changed his will and was donating the farm to Ohio State for agricultural studies. My inheritance! Given away just like that so some kid could study soil conservation or crap. What about me? What was I going to get? Nothing, that's what. Not a plug nickel."

"Is that when you hit him?" I asked. I shook my head at the terrible waste of life caused by greed.

"Yeah, I guess so. I saw red and just grabbed the shovel from his hand and swung it. It happened in a blur. When I heard that guy

184

coming, that scout leader, I ducked into the corn stalks before I had a chance to find the key in his pocket," Allen explained sullenly.

"What's so important about this key?" questioned Doug as he examined the key now in his possession.

"Opens the safe deposit box in the bank. I needed to destroy that new will before anyone saw it. I had to try to protect what was mine."

"Don't you know that your father's lawyer probably has a copy of the new will? Destroying one copy won't change anything. You did it all for nothing," Doug told him.

"Take him away," Sheriff Simmons directed disgustedly. "And you, young woman," wagging a finger at me, "better stay out of police business next time," the sheriff admonished.

"Next time?" I laughed.

"Oh, no! Don't get any ideas. Let's go find our boy and go home," said Doug as he grabbed my hand and we slowly walked up the steps and headed outside.

Billy stood next to Ida Cooper as the paramedics loaded her husband into an ambulance. He spotted us and ran cheerfully to our waiting arms. I hugged him to me; tears filled my eyes and ran down my cheeks at the sight of him.

"Aww, Mom, you're squishing me," Billy complained.

"I'm so proud of you. You were very brave, and you got help."

Doug enveloped us in a group hug, then started to laugh.

"You two look like a pair of chimney sweeps," he said as he pointed to our tear-streaked, sooty faces.

"What's a chimney sweep?" asked Billy.

Local newspapers and television news stations described the exciting details and events leading up to the capture of Allen Granger. Delegated to page three of the Columbus Dispatch, a three-column story posted the story about the capture of Harry Logan by the Michigan State Police as he tried to sneak across the border into Canada. Michigan will extradite him back to Ohio for arrest and trial for the funds he embezzled. The Knox Savings and Loan planned to return as much money as possible to the victim accounts and credit all property taxes as paid in full. No evictions or sheriff sales.

I read the headlines once again and reached for the ringing telephone for the umpteenth time that day. Mittens jumped down from his perch on a kitchen bar stool and gave me a look that clearly conveyed he did not like all this commotion.

"Hello. Oh, hi Aunt Fran. Mm-hmm, yeah, come on over."

I hung up the phone, wondering what that was all about. Guess I better put on a fresh pot of coffee. Anna and my aunt would be here in ten minutes.

No sooner had the coffee stopped perking than the back door opened with Aunt Fran and Anna striding into the cozy kitchen.

"Look what I brought for our famous hero of the day," beamed Anna as she placed one of Martha's Bakery famous apple cobblers on the countertop.

186

"Oh my, we are indulging," I said as I reached for small plates and forks. "Coffee?"

"Love a cup. Got a pitcher of milk?" asked Anna as she helped herself to the refrigerator and found what she was looking for.

I poured three mugs of hot fresh coffee while Aunt Fran sliced the cobbler and spooned some onto each plate. The cinnamon and nutmeg fragrances enticed our waiting palettes.

"I walked past the butcher shop this morning on my way to Martha's and looked through the front windows. The place is empty; not a single pork chop or piece of chicken in the case. I mean the shop appears totally deserted," Anna declared.

"That's what I wanted to talk to you both about. I have something to tell you, but you must promise this goes no further than this kitchen," Aunt Fran stated as she took a sip of her coffee.

"What's going on?" I asked. I ate a forkful of the delicious cobbler and savored the flavor. "Mmm."

"You recall I had a date with Sam on Saturday night? We had a wonderful dinner and evening. Let's just say that I haven't enjoyed that type of manly attention in a long, long while," Aunt Fran sighed before continuing quietly. "Sam has left town."

"What? Why?" I asked, surprised. "Am I the reason, all my snooping?" Now I felt guilty and really bad for upsetting Aunt Fran's relationship. She obviously liked the guy.

"No, but all the media attention in town what with the bank thefts and the murder of Fred Granger and then Allen's capture... well, that

187

sort of worried Sam. When he was questioned by the police too, it became a problem. The Feds were afraid Sam might be interviewed on TV or something and he'd be recognized."

"Feds... what are we talking about here?" I asked.

"Sam told me Saturday night that he was leaving; we were in bed and he asked me to go with him. For a split second I really wanted to, but you know, I told him I couldn't. My family and friends are here, and my business. I can't just pull up stakes and take off," Aunt Fran explained in a low voice.

"Wait a minute. You said you were in bed?" Anna interjected.

"Forget that, I want to know more about these Feds," I said.

"Sam swore me to secrecy but told me he's in witness protection. The U.S. Marshalls came in early Sunday and literally packed him up and moved him to a new location. He'll get a new name and identity, job, everything. He can't contact me ever again and I don't know where he went."

"Holy cow. No wonder I couldn't find out any information on Sam Tilley when I did a Google search. I always thought it weird that he just didn't exist before Meadowood, and now I know why. Was he really a witness or some kind of mob boss?" I wondered.

"He couldn't tell me more than that, but I think he was an important witness in some case, so that's why he's under federal protection," Aunt Fran said, dabbing at moist eyes.

"I'm sorry. I know you were fond of him. Someday you'll meet another nice man," commented Anna. She patted Fran's arm.

I squeezed my aunt's hand and kissed her cheek lightly. She was still a vibrant, lovely woman and deserved some happiness in her life. I made a mental promise to myself that I'd always support her choices wherever life took her.

"I'm glad you'll have a special memory of your time with Sam," I said as I hugged her again.

"Thank you both. I wanted you to know what really happened. The Marshalls have already spread some kind of story or rumor about town to explain his departure and all the food in the butcher shop was donated to the county soup kitchen." Fran wiped away her tears and smiled; she clapped her hands once, then placed them on the counter as she leaned forward. "So, girls, let's talk about our food drive and what we need to do next for the needy at Christmas."

I smiled and shook my head. I can just imagine my calendar filling up with future meetings and community events with these two involved ladies. Meadowood sure keeps me busy; I may have to change my opinion of my little town.

Author Biography

A resident of central Ohio for over 40 years; Nancy M. Wade and her husband Gary now claim the hills of N.E. Tennessee as home. Nancy is an active member of the Lost State Writer's Guild in the Tri-City area. She is a graduate of East Tennessee State University.

Her works combine romance and mystery with warm characters set in historic timeframes and locales or cozy, small town settings.

Nancy M. Wade's novels include the romantic suspense Circle-D Sagas: _Endless Circle_ and _Moment in Time;_ a rich family drama, _Reflections: A Sentimental Journey;_ a historical romance novel, _Frontier Heart;_ plus, a contemporary short story called _Courtship of Laura._ Her cozy mystery series titled _A Meadowood Mystery_ includes: _Scarecrows and Corpses_ , _Reunion with Death, Deadly Bones, and Berry Little Murder._ All her books are available for order online in both paperback or E-book formats on Barnes & Noble, Books-a-Million, Amazon.com, and IngramSpark.

A Note from the Author

I hope you enjoyed reading **Scarecrows and Corpses**. If you would like to leave a review, please go to www.amazon.com or www.goodreads.com and do so today. I love hearing what readers have to say about my stories and characters.

Connect with me on social media on Instagram or with my Facebook page: https://www.facebook.com/authorNancyMWade/ Follow my blog & explore my web site: https://nancymwade.com

**Thank you! Nancy Wade**

www.ingramcontent.com/pod-product-compliance
Lightning Source LLC
Chambersburg PA
CBHW070354200726
48294CB00003B/905